Under the Watchful Moon

By Amy Klco

Enchantment Press
Under the Watchful Moon
Published by Enchantment Press
Hessel, Michigan 49745

ISBN: 978-0-9979511-5-8

0 9 8 7 6 5 4 3 2 1

To Paul Goddard,
Forever and always, in this lifetime,
and every lifetime to come.

Author's Note:

This book is a work of fiction, but as they always say, "write what you know." Some of it is, I'll admit, based on my own experiences. Some of it is based on stories I've been told by others. And some of it is just made up. Please do not assume that what you read is fact. My mother used to say "don't air your dirty laundry in public." But as Steven Saylor said, "All writing is an act of self-exploration." So I will hang my dirty laundry up, along with clothes that aren't even mine. My biggest hope is that this book will help you to air out some of your own laundry, as well.

If you or someone you know is in an abusive relationship, you can get help by calling the National Domestic Violence Hotline at 1-800-799-7233.

Chapter 1

I watched her, as she drove the new-old pickup truck, filled with everything she had left in the world, and I felt so much pride—for everything she had made it through, for getting the strength to start over, and for all the things that were yet to come in her life. I wished I could tell her what the future would bring, but all I could do was shine down on her and wish her well...

Rachel rode on into the night, knowing what she had left behind but not really sure where she was going. Her destination: the upper peninsula of Michigan, near a small town on the coast of Lake Superior. There was a house there—more of a cabin, really—that she had rented without ever seeing it in person. She had fallen in love with the pictures of it on the internet. The description said it was "one of the oldest standing buildings in the area." Rachel knew it was the perfect place for her new life.

It wasn't as close to her new job—as a teacher in a Native American school—as was really practical. She had heard all the stories of the bitter winters in the U.P. and of the lake-effect snows that could prevent her from even leaving the driveway at times. If she had been more practical, she would have found a home in town where, if the snows were too bad to drive in, she could always just walk to work. That would have been the responsible thing to do.

But Rachel was tired of doing the "responsible" thing. Her whole life, she had been the responsible one. Even as a child, when her mother had been bed-ridden with overwhelming depression, it was Rachel who took care of her and her younger brother, Timmy. It was like she had been a mother since the day she was born—or at least since the day he was born nine years later. Which is why it was so ironic that she never actually was a mother. Well, that wasn't totally true. For six months, as her daughter grew inside of her, she was a mother to it. Until that fateful day, and those stairs, and... But that was another story. And so long ago. And now, for the first time ever, Rachel was not responsible for anyone but herself.

It was a wonderful feeling—and also scary as hell. What would she do with herself? How would she spend her time? And how would she be able to feel that she was worth anything at all, if she wasn't busy taking care of someone else?

Sure, there was the teaching, of course. If nothing else, her job as a teacher would insure that she always had someone to take care of. And things to do—lessons to plan and papers to correct. But even with that, what would she do if she suddenly found herself with that elusive concept she had never really known before: free time?

She lived with her mother throughout her college years, commuting to classes and doing her homework at night, after Timmy was in bed. No dorm life for her, no college parties or clubs or extra activities. She did try out for a play once, but then declined the part she was offered when she realized there was no way she could fit rehearsals into her schedule. Because if she wasn't home at night, who was going to make sure Timmy got his dinner, or Mom, for that matter? The fun times would just have to wait—Rachel would have to wait. And wait she did. Until Timmy—who went by Tim now—left for college himself. Then Rachel found a nice nursing home for her mom, the nicest she could afford with her mom's disability checks, anyway. Only then, once she knew everyone else was taken care of, did Rachel allow herself to have some fun.

The "fun" lasted all of about a month. That's how long it took Rachel to meet Frank. And move in with him. And trade her role of mother-to-her-mother to that of wife.

As she rode through the moonlit night on the way to a

new life, Rachel pondered, again, what had first attracted her to Frank. Perhaps it was the fun that he seemed to offer. She met him at the bar, a place she had never allowed herself to go before Tim left for school. He'd offered to buy her a drink. They'd danced. She found herself telling him her life story. And he seemed genuinely interested in hearing it.

That was what it was, Rachel realized with sudden clarity. He made her feel special. And in turn, she did everything she could to make him feel special, too. She drove him to his apartment that night, since he was too drunk to drive. She tucked him in and spent a wakeful night on his couch, listening to his fitful sleep. She didn't dare leave him alone in that condition.

When he woke up, he thanked her for taking care of him. He made her pancakes. Then he took her to his bed. And she never left it again.

Not until tonight, Rachel thought with a laugh. For the first time in ten years, she would sleep alone tonight. And every night from here on out, she vowed. Never again would she let her heart trick her as it had done with Frank. He was the only man she had ever been with—but she had no desire for another. Never again! "Perhaps there is such a thing as true love," Rachel speculated, not ready to give up all hope. "But not for me. For me, the best that I can hope for is to just be free. And at this moment, freedom feels better than love ever could!"

She reached the cabin well past midnight. The key had been placed above the doorsill, just as her new landlord had promised it would be. She let herself in. After a long, emotional day, she would have liked to just crawl into bed and go to sleep. But there were a few problems with that plan—the first being that she didn't have a bed to climb into. The cabin was unfurnished and the bed she'd shared with Frank for the last ten years had stayed behind with him. But she did have a sleeping bag, which she pulled out of the truck cab and set down by the fireplace. Tomorrow, perhaps, she could locate a resale shop and start searching for furniture. But for tonight, there were more pressing matters.

The biggest one being the fireplace. Or more specifically, what was not yet in the fireplace—a fire. Although it was August, there was a chill to the air—perhaps from the wind that blew off of Lake Superior. The cabin had been fitted with electricity, thank goodness, along with plumbing and electric baseboard heaters. But it also had a fireplace (complete with insert) because, as the landlord had pointed out, "trying to heat with just electricity will cost you an arm and a leg. Keep the thermostat at fifty-five degrees, so the pipes don't freeze. But if you want it any warmer than that, your best bet is to build a fire. I'll even leave you a seasoned face cord of wood, split and stacked, in the rack next to the cabin. That will get you started, at least." Rachel didn't know what "seasoned" or "face cord" meant, but what she did understand was that there was some wood already there for her to use. She went outside, located the rack of firewood covering almost the whole side of the cabin, grabbed an armful, and went back inside.

She thought back to the days before Timmy was born, before their father had left them. Back when she was eight years old and she had been in Girl Scouts. A lot of their time had been spent with crafts and songs and mostly just giggling. But they had learned the basics of how to start a fire. "Start with some kindling. Then a few small sticks. Don't add the big logs until the fire really starts to go." Rachel spoke these words aloud to herself, glad there was no one else there to hear her, even more glad that there was no one else there to tell her she was doing it wrong.

It took her a while to get the fire going—it had been so long since those days in Girl Scouts. And yet, it also felt natural for her to be doing it. "Is it like riding a bicycle?" she thought aloud. "Once you have learned it, does it come back without even thinking?"

Then she laughed. "And now I am talking to myself," she added. "Is this the first sign of madness?" But it wasn't madness at all, she knew. If she didn't speak to herself, who would? She was so unused to the silence that it made her uncomfortable. Even her own voice was better than no sound at all.

Once the fire was finally going and properly stoked with a big log, Rachel unfolded her sleeping bag and laid it down next to the fire. She bunched up a sweatshirt to use as a pillow and snuggled in for some much needed sleep.

That sleep was short and fitful. Rachel woke up at dawn—after only about four hours—sore and freezing cold. The fire was out.

"What was I thinking?" she cursed herself, as she pulled on her winter coat and started the fire-building process all over again. Yes, she could have just turned the thermostat up, but if she was going to do this cabin-thing, she was determined to do it right from the start. Still, that didn't mean she wasn't going to question herself at times.

"Why did I choose to live out here, in this 'picturesque' cabin instead of finding a nice place in town? Somewhere with the modern conveniences, like a furnace?" Rachel laughed, not entirely good-naturedly, at her own folly. For it had been foolish to decide to live in what was basically a summer cabin, all year round, in a part of the state that was known for its bitter winters. If she hadn't been such an idiot, she would have chosen better.

"You really are as stupid as Frank says you are!" Rachel thought, then caught herself, remembering what the books had said. She didn't need to buy into Frank's opinion anymore. She didn't need to believe that she was dumb or that she was crazy, as Frank had told her time and time again. It wasn't true. In fact, Rachel knew, Frank didn't even really believe it was true. According to the books that Rachel had read (staying late at work to read them since she didn't dare bring them into the house,) he had told her those things in order to control her. Gaslighting, they called it, when you convinced someone else that their perception of reality was wrong, so that you could get them to believe your version—make them think they are crazy so they will believe whatever you tell them. Rachel thought with sympathy of the woman in the movie that the term had been coined from, about how the gas lights in her home would turn dim when her husband was in the attic, doing things he shouldn't be. And how, when she tried to tell him about it, he denied it, telling her it was all in her head.

How many times had Rachel heard that phrase? "It's all in your head!" Frank had told her time and time again. "I would never really hurt you. I don't know what you are making a big deal about." Rachel, often still nursing bruises from his beating the night before, was inclined to believe him. After all, it wasn't like he'd meant to hurt her. She should have known better than to make him upset when he'd been drinking. If only she had a better idea of just what would make him upset.

Rachel had believed his story without question for years, until the day she was six months pregnant, the day they had stood on the stairs outside their third-floor apartment and gotten into a fight. Rachel called their "discussions" fights, but they really weren't. A fight implied that both parties were arguing back and forth. But Rachel never argued with Frank. She just listened to his rage. If she had spoken up, she knew, it would have only made it worse.

Thinking back on it now, in the cold cabin as she struggled to build a fire, Rachel couldn't remember what the "fight" had been about. But she remembered every other detail of that day. It was early spring. There was a slight chill to the air, but after a long winter, it felt warm enough to be outside without a coat on. Frank was yelling at her, but in her memory of it, she couldn't hear his voice. It was like watching TV with the volume off. What she could hear was the sound of a bird chirping in the distance, thankful as she was for the spring. She smelled mud. She felt her daughter move inside her, stretching. And then suddenly she was falling, tumbling head over heels down the stairs. She remembered hitting the first landing and continuing down. Then all went black.

When she woke up later, in the hospital, the nurse told her that she had lost the baby and that her uterus had detached from her fallopian tubes, preventing any more babies in the future. And then she gave Rachel the books.

Books on alcoholism. Books on breaking free of abusive relationships. Books on codependency. Rachel took them, hid them in her suitcase, and then smuggled them to school as soon as she could. It would take her two more years before she even dared to open one and start to read it. And even more years before she had the courage to act on what she'd read and finally leave him.

"Thank you," Rachel now said aloud to the nurse whose name she no longer remembered. "I am a bit slow, but I can learn. And I have no doubt that you saved my life with those books. Because if I hadn't left..."

Rachel shuddered, only partly from the cold. More from the memory of the day before, when Rachel finally told Frank she was leaving. She had made all her plans in secret—applying for a new teaching job over the internet, renting the cabin sight unseen, stashing away whatever money she could. She bought an old blue Ford truck for only three hundred dollars. She wasn't even sure if it would make it all the way to the cabin. But there was enough room in the back for the few possessions Rachel couldn't stand to leave behind. A bookshelf her dad had made long ago. A small trunk that had been her great-aunt's. Books. Some clothes. And an antique, cast-iron, treadle sewing machine.

Now Rachel laughed, remembering how she had waited for Frank to leave the house that day. As soon as she was sure he really was gone, she went to get the truck from down the road, where she had parked it out of his sight. And then she had, by herself, wrestled each item onto the truck bed. The sewing machine had been a trick, but she found that if she propped one corner onto the tailgate, she could kind of roll it over itself the rest of the way. Not the ideal way to do it, but it got the job done.

It would have been nice to have someone to help her, a friend or neighbor, but Rachel had no one. Frank had seen to that, too. Any time Rachel had tried to make friends or reach out to someone she knew in the past, Frank had pushed them away. Sometimes slyly, by hinting to Rachel that they were only using her for her money or her friendship or her help. Sometimes, he scared them away with straight-on threats, saying what he would do to them if they didn't stay away from his wife. Either way, the results were the same. Rachel had no friends she could turn to. Even Timmy had been erased from her life, when Frank had made her choose between him or her brother. She hadn't spoken to Timmy, now, in over three years.

So Rachel had loaded up the truck alone, securing a tarp over it all in case of rain. And then she sat down and waited for her husband to come home, so she could break the news to him. It was one of his bar nights, but she knew he would stop home, first, to get ready.

Perhaps it would have been smarter to just leave. Write a note saying goodbye and be long gone before he got home. But despite it all, Rachel couldn't bring herself to do that. She had to face him. She had to give him the courtesy of her honesty, even if he had never been honest with her.

He was honest now, telling her exactly how he felt about her. With words. And with his hands around her throat. Did he plan to kill her, to strangle her there and then so she couldn't leave? Or was he just trying to hold her in place long enough for him to say everything he wanted to say? Rachel didn't wait to find out. She kneed him squarely between the legs and then ran out the door and into her truck before he had a chance to recover. Her last sight of her husband was him chasing after her, yelling, "You can't leave me! You can't!"

But, as Rachel realized with a laugh, she could. And she did.

"Now what?" she asked herself, as she finally got the fire burning again. She had gotten this far, mostly just by sheer strength of will. But what was she going to do now that she was here? Today and the rest of her life?

"Today," she told herself, "You will unpack. Then you will go into town and see about getting a bed and maybe even a chair, table, and shower curtain. As for the rest of your life, well, that will sort itself out in time. You have two weeks before school starts," she reminded herself. "Two weeks to turn this cabin into a home. That is your focus right now." And with that, she began the process of unloading her truck and planning what she should look to buy when she went into town.

"Let's see," she said as she worked. "I need a bed, clearly. And sheets, a comforter, and a pillow. A dresser would be good, too. I can use my sewing machine as a desk, but I'll need a chair to sit on. A couch would be nice. And some kind of kitchen table. Oh, and while I'm in town, I'd better pick up some food. It will be weird," she noted, "cooking for one. I can actually make what I want, instead of just cooking what Frank wants."

It felt strange, saying his name in this cabin, so far away from where he was. But Rachel also knew that it would not be the last time she said it. Although she had left him and had gained the courage to start a life without him by her side, Rachel realized, almost instinctively, that he wasn't gone from her life yet. Perhaps he never totally would be. He was too much a part of her mind now, too much a part of the way she thought and acted, to be erased as easily as that. It would take more than a three-hundred-mile drive to rid her of his influence on her life.

"But," she resolved, "that doesn't mean I'm not going to try."

It was late by the time she returned from town. Her "hunt" had been successful—more so than she had even hoped it would be. At a large charity store, she'd found a twin bed, complete with mattress, for only thirty dollars. They also had a hide-a-bed couch for fifteen. The material—a ghastly yellow floral pattern—was stained and starting to fray at the arms, but Rachel thought that perhaps she could learn how to reupholster it. For now, it could be covered with a sheet. And the best part was that one of the workers helped her to load the items in the back of her truck.

She also found a small second-hand store where she bought some of the other things she would need, such as the bed sheets and comforter, towels, pots and pans, and a set of antique china dishes. It seemed rather an extravagant purchase, but she did need something to eat off of and they were offering the whole twenty-piece set for only five dollars. It would have cost her more to buy just one place setting new.

Antique items had always brought her a certain joy. Frank never understood this. He had picked on her time and again about her sewing machine, which he said "just took up space. It's not like you even know how to sew!"

"Perhaps I will learn how," Rachel replied to the phantom of his voice. "Now that I have some time to do what I want."

But she hadn't bought the sewing machine—or protected it from his numerous attempts to throw it out—so she could sew on it. There was something about just looking at it that comforted her, made her feel at home in a world that, for the most part, she never really felt as if she belonged in. It just felt right to have it in her life, just as now it felt right to own a set of china dishes. And to be living in a cabin in the middle of nowhere, heated by a wood fire. Maybe not the easy way to go but the right way.

She didn't change her mind on that, even when she got back home and unloaded the parts of her new bed. It wasn't until she tried to move her new couch that she realized that a life alone, "in the middle of nowhere," might have some drawbacks. She'd had help at the store, getting it onto her truck bed. But now, she wasn't so sure how she was going to get it off and into the house.

"You idiot!" she heard Frank's voice in her head. "You didn't think of that, did you? What's your great plan now?"

Rachel wasn't going to let Frank—or the phantom of him that lived in her mind—make her feel foolish for buying the hide-a-bed. It was a good deal and it would be nice to have, placed by the fire, where she could cuddle under a blanket on those infamous cold winter's nights. She could even pull out the bed if she had company (someday, she vowed, she would have friends and they would come to visit and then the hide-a-bed would be perfect.) For now, she would, somehow, find a way to get it inside.

She reached for one end and pulled it to the edge of the tailgate. "Maybe I can tip it down and set the end on the ground," Rachel thought, pulling the end just a little further out. "I'll just pivot it up in the air and..."

As the main part of the sofa came off the truck, the center of gravity shifted, the full weight of the couch came crashing down on Rachel, and Rachel came crashing down on the ground, pinned beneath it.

It was there, peeking out from under the end of the sofa, that she first saw James.

"I thought I'd better come check to see how my new tenant was settling in," James said, by way of introduction, as he climbed out of his truck.

Rachel recognized his voice, since she had spoken to him several times on the phone. Her new landlord. And yet, his voice had not given her any indication of just how blue his eyes were, or how tenderly they would look at her.

"Something told me you might need some help getting things all set up," James said with a laugh. "I guess I was right!"

Rachel felt embarrassed at being found in such a circumstance. As was often the case when she found herself in a situation where she needed help, Rachel felt herself close up, her indignation erecting walls instantaneously.

"I don't need help from you or any other man!" she snapped at him. "I am doing just fine." She tried to wiggle out from under the couch, managing to tip it just enough for the hide-a-bed to pop out—covering her further.

James, carefully suppressing a chuckle, wasn't at all put

off by her attitude. "The fact that I'm a man has nothing to do with it," he said as he flipped the couch over and off her. "But sometimes, having an extra set of hands, no matter whose hands they are, can be helpful." He reached out, then, and offered his hand to Rachel, to help her up.

Rachel reached out for his, but as soon as their hands touched, something happened.

Have you ever been walking along, minding your own business, when suddenly the world seemed to tilt slightly, as if your sense of perspective had been off and now it was righting itself? This happened to Rachel from time to time, just often enough to make her wonder if something was wrong with her. Vertigo or something like that. But this time, when things shifted, it was like her world had come unglued. And she was no longer where she had been the moment before.

She was still on the ground, but that ground was muddier than before. The truck beside her had changed, too, into a wooden wagon. The man in front of her looked the same, although younger, and his clothing had changed. He wore a cream-colored shirt and brown pants, held up with suspenders. On his head was an ivy cap, like the kind that you would see on a kid in a Charles Dickens' play.

"Beg your pardon, ma'am," he was saying as he helped her stand up. "I didn't see you there."

She allowed this man to help her stand, steadying herself on her high-heeled boots. She shook her skirts to readjust them, before even realizing what she was doing.

"My name is Jebediah," he told her, still holding her hand. "I work over at the lumber mill," he added. "And you must be Mistress Annie, the new school teacher. It's a pleasure to meet you." He pulled her hand to his lips and kissed it before finally letting it go.

"The pleasure is mine," Rachel—or was it Annie—said. "But I really must be going now," she added.

"Of course," the strange man named Jebediah replied. "You have a lot to do to get the schoolhouse ready before the pupils show up tomorrow." And with that, he tipped his cap at her and left.

She watched him go, only turning around after he was out of sight to realize that she was standing in front of a one-room schoolhouse, just like the one from the *Little House on the Prairie* television show she had loved to watch as a girl. But how was any of this possible?

As soon as that question entered her brain, the world shifted again, and Rachel found that she was back in her own world, back in her own shoes as it were, standing next to James, her landlord, who was looking at her a bit perplexedly. "Are you back with us now?" he asked.

Rachel could only nod, not sure what words she could use to explain what had just happened. Not sure, to be honest, if there was any way to explain what had happened. Or if it had really happened at all.

"Then let's move this couch inside," James replied, quite business-like. "It should be a bit easier if we work together. Although," he added with a wink, "I have no doubt that you would have found a way to do it on your own, if you had to."

Rachel didn't like that wink. It made her feel... well, never mind how it made her feel. It didn't matter, anyway. She knew who she was now, and she wasn't going to give that up for any man, even one with eyes as blue as the nearby lake.

And, as I sometimes do, I snuck into the sky before the sun had even set, peeking through the branches to see those two, finding each other once again. She wasn't quite ready for him yet, but he could wait a little longer. He had already waited so long.

James had moved to the U.P. almost three decades ago, when Rachel was still a child living at home. He never really meant to move to the U.P. He came up to help his brother start a business. After that, he planned to leave, maybe move to California or New Orleans. But one opportunity after another had presented itself and he had stayed, waiting for someone he could build a life with. The women that he met were insecure. Or shallow. Or didn't love him back. They didn't want to build a life with him— they just cared about what life he could give to them.

So he made a life for himself. He owned a restaurant for a while. And a store. Finally he had settled into real estate. It allowed him to make a living for himself without having to be at work twenty-four/seven. And it gave him time to do his woodworking.

At heart, James was a carpenter, and he loved nothing better than to be in his shop, restoring old furniture. Or repurposing old furniture into new items that had the charm of yesteryear and the practicality of today.

He sold much of his work, for a price probably much lower than it was worth. But he didn't do it for the money. He did it because he loved to watch old things become new again, to save these items and turn them into something someone could love. And knowing that they were going to someone who really did love them was the best reward for his labors.

James noticed Rachel's old sewing machine as they were struggling with the couch. A pretty piece of work, but James' practiced eye also noticed the water stain on the lid and the places where the veneer was starting to chip. "I'd like the chance to fix it up," he thought, then laughed at himself. Yes, he wanted the chance to fix up that old sewing machine. But that wasn't all he wanted to fix up. If being single into his fifties had taught him nothing else, it had taught him how to know when a woman was hurting. And it didn't take much to see that Rachel was hurting.

"No," he said to himself, sternly this time. "It is not my job to take on this project—either of these projects. I have had enough of helping women feel better about themselves, only to have them leave me once they do. Besides," he added. "She must be at least ten years younger than me. I'd better just stay away."

Which is what he did, for many turns of my cycle. Which was just as well, because Rachel was busy finding herself—and learning to remember her past self—again. But they had met, now. And when she was finally ready, I would make sure that their paths crossed again.

After all, these two were destined to be together, not just in this lifetime, but in every life. They would be reborn, forgetting everything. But each time, with my help, they would find each other again, whether it happened right away or decades down the road. Because, although they might forget the person, they would never lose the longing for each other. And that longing would always bring them together in the end.

Chapter 2

The experience she had when she took James' hand, of time suddenly changing, stayed with Rachel for days. As she began to set up her classroom in her new school, she would think back to the one-room schoolhouse she had seen. As she set up the laptop cart in her room, she wondered if Annie would have been expected to provide her students with slates, or if they would have brought their own from home. And what about books? And what would the curriculum have been like back then? Would she really have focused on teaching the students the "three R's": reading, writing, and arithmetic? What would her pupils have been like? Instead of thinking of her own incoming students, Rachel found herself fascinated by the thought of learning more about who Annie's students would have been.

She often stopped by the second-hand store on her way back to the cabin. She liked going there. She never knew what deals she might find, and the storeowner was a nice old man who loved to talk. And for Rachel, who had no one else to talk to, it was nice to listen to his stories.

"You might find this interesting," the owner said to her one day, "since you're a teacher." He handed her an old McGuffey's primer, one of the most common books used to teach children in the late nineteenth and early twentieth centuries. Surely this was the kind of book Annie would have used to teach her students.

As Rachel took the book from the store owner's hands, she felt her world shift again. She was inside the class-room—not her classroom, but Annie's. There were wooden desks, all lined up in rows, where children sat, staring up at her—fifteen in all, she quickly counted, ranging in age from what looked like about five up to about fourteen. Annie looked out at these faces, staring up at her, and was overcome with fear. How was she going to teach them? Each one was so different, each one had their own needs. She wanted to help them all, but could she? Could she even get them to treat her as a proper teacher? She was, after all, not much older than some of them.

"Let's start off by getting to know each other," Annie began. "My name is Miss Annie. I love reading and learning, and I hope that by the end of the year, you will, too."

"Is this your first time teaching?" one of the boys in back asked.

"Well, yes it is," Annie admitted. *A fool's mistake,* Rachel—observing this whole thing through Annie's eyes—noted. *Never tell the kids you haven't been a teacher before. They will eat you alive!* "But I am sure you guys will be able to help me figure it all out," Annie added.

"Well," said another older boy. "You should let us decide what subjects we want to study and when. And we will need lots of recess breaks. Oh, and you can never give us any homework."

"Don't listen to the Thompson twins, Miss Annie," Sissy Wallace—the young girl who lived at the farm where Annie was boarding—spoke up. "They are just trying to trick you. But if they give you any trouble, you just tell their pa and he'll set them right."

"I appreciate the suggestion," Annie told the young girl, dreading to think exactly how the Thompson twins' father would "set them right." She vowed to herself to only call home as a last resort.

Call? Annie thought, surprised at her own words. *On the telephone?* They didn't have a telephone at the farm where she was boarding. And she doubted very highly that the Thomson family had one, either. In fact, the only telephone she knew about in town was at the general store. If you wanted to make a call—and you knew someone else who had a phone that you could call—you would have to have the whole discussion in front of any other customer who happened to come along. *Why, then, had she thought about calling these boys' father?*

"Are you alright?" the storekeeper asked Rachel, jolting her out of her trance.

"Um, sorry," Rachel mumbled. "Just a lot on my mind right now," she added.

"Of course," the store owner assured her. "You said you were a teacher, right? And school is starting again soon. Are you looking forward to it?" Before Rachel could even answer him, he continued, "I remember when I was a kid, I was always nervous about the first day. But not, I suppose, more than the teacher was. I only had one person I had to try to impress. But you have a whole classroom full of kids to make a first impression with. What grade did you say you taught?"

"Fifth," Rachel replied.

"Fifth grade, huh? I remember that age—old enough to feel like you were the king of the school. But then you went to middle school and that all changed."

"I like that age," Rachel explained. She always felt like she had to explain why she liked teaching that age, instead of the cute little ones. "They are old enough to have some pretty amazing conversations with. But they are still young enough to get excited about things. I taught high school for one year, and that was tiring. I swear, they spent the whole time trying to convince their friends that they didn't care about anything. At least, not anything the teacher was telling them."

"Well, teenagers, you know?" the storekeeper said, as if that explained everything. In a way, it did.

Rachel made one other stop in town before she went home and got herself a cell phone. She'd had one, of course, when she'd lived with Frank. He had insisted on it, and had further insisted that she keep it with her at all times, so he could get ahold of her at any moment if he needed to. He had also required that she keep the location service active, so he always knew where she was. Which is why, when she left that day, she left the phone behind. She didn't want a leash tying her to him anymore.

On the other hand, even out in the middle of nowhere— perhaps especially because she was out in the middle of nowhere—she needed to have some way to contact others. For one thing, she needed to start calling around, looking for a lawyer to take her case. Leaving Frank was a good first step, but she knew things weren't really over until she got a divorce.

The first call she made on her new cell phone—after using some of her new data plan to find the number—was to her brother. She had missed him a lot in the three years since she had broken off ties with him. Why, she wondered now, had she chosen Frank over Timmy? Surely, anyone who would make her choose between them and her own family was someone she didn't really want to be with, right?

But to be honest, she hadn't really had a choice—or at least she hadn't felt like she had. She wasn't afraid that Frank would hurt her for it. When he did hurt her, physically, there was never any real cause. As she told herself in an effort to excuse his actions, it wasn't Frank that was hurting her—it was the alcohol. But the physical pain wasn't what scared Rachel into cutting ties with her brother.

Her real fear, as crazy as it sounded, was that she would hurt Frank. She did love him and she had vowed to love him "for better or for worse," forever. But he never seemed to believe her.

"You care more about your snotty little brother than you do about me!" he accused her. "I knew you didn't really love me. You're just like the rest of them."

And Rachel sobbed and told him that wasn't true, that she did love him, that she loved him more than anything. Then she called her brother and said she never wanted to talk to him again. Anything to make sure Frank knew how much she loved him. Anything to help him see that she cared. Because maybe, if he could finally see that she really did love him, maybe he could stop the drinking. Maybe he could finally turn his life around and they could be happy together, the way it was supposed to be.

The way, Rachel finally saw, that it never would be, because it was not the way Frank wanted it to be. He didn't want to quit drinking. He didn't want to "turn his life around." That would mean he would have had to take control of his own life. And he preferred it when his wife did that for him.

All this ran through Rachel's mind as she dialed her brother's number, listened to the ringing, and waited to see if he would answer. After five rings, she was about to give up when she heard a voice on the other side. "Hello?" it said. "Who is this?"

"Timmy...Tim," Rachel said, filled with relief. "It's me. Rachel. Your sister. I...I..." but she couldn't say anymore. She was crying too hard.

"Rachel?" she heard his voice say. "Is that really you? Are you okay? It's been so long."

"I...I left Frank," she said between sobs. There was nothing else to say, nothing else that needed to be said.

On the other end of the phone, Tim let out a sigh of relief. "Thank God," he replied. "I was so worried for you. But you wouldn't talk to me and there was nothing I could do and..." Tim stopped suddenly. "Are you okay,

Rachel? He didn't hurt you before you left, did he? He's not chasing you down or anything, is he?"

Rachel laughed, but then realized it was a fair question, all things considered. "No, he didn't hurt me," she replied, only fudging the truth a little. "And I don't think he's chasing me down. I'm going to call a lawyer tomorrow and see what I have to do to get an official divorce. But I had to get out. And I had to talk to you. It's been so long and... but enough about me. How have you been doing?"

They talked for almost two hours before Tim finally had to say goodbye. As Rachel set down her new cell phone, she smiled and said a tiny prayer to the Universe. "Thank you, whoever or whatever you are. I thought I was all alone. But now I know that I'm not. I have someone who loves me, someone who really cares about my happiness. And what a difference that makes!"

School started and Rachel found that she liked her coworkers, she liked her boss, she even liked her students. But one thing had changed in her. In the past, she had always been known as having the "patience of a saint." No matter what a kid did, she never lost her composure. In fact, she had been accused at times of being "too nice." Now, Rachel found that she didn't have quite the same patience. When she asked a student to do something and they didn't—which happens often with kids—she'd find herself getting angry. She'd raise her voice, she would send the student out of the room, and sometimes, she would even send them down to the principal's office. This wasn't like her and it really bothered her.

Finally, after one really hard day, Rachel stopped by the school counselor. "Do you have a few minutes to talk?" she asked.

The counselor, an attractive, classy older woman, motioned her to come in and shut the door. "I have as much time as you need," she told Rachel.

Which was good, because Rachel was there for over an hour. At first, Rachel wasn't sure what to say. But once she started, it all came tumbling out. The concern about her lack of patience with her students. But then, the rest came out, too. About leaving Frank. About why she left Frank. About losing the baby. About the books. About the pain he had caused her for so long—physical pain, yes, but also all the emotional pain.

All the strength Rachel had on the day she'd left him, the strength that had gotten her through the first month on her own, now left her. Before long, she was sobbing like a baby.

The counselor offered her some Kleenex. She held her hand and let her talk—and cry—as long as she needed to.

"I'm sorry," Rachel said when she was finally back in control. "I'm sorry for taking up so much of your time."

"Nonsense," the counselor replied. "You needed someone to talk to. My job is to be here for anyone who needs to talk. You can come to me anytime you need."

"Thank you, Mrs. Jacobs," Rachel said, remembering how the students referred to her.

"Call me Sara," she replied. "I think we can be on a first name basis now." She smiled. "And Rachel, do me a favor. Give yourself a break, okay? You are going through a lot right now. You are re-learning how to live your life for yourself, for once. That takes time."

"But the students," Rachel said, thinking back to what had originally brought her into Sara's office. "Why am I so impatient with them all of a sudden?"

Instead of answering, Sara asked her another question. "Did your husband do what you asked him to?"

"Never," Rachel admitted. "In fact, he would get angry if I asked him to do anything. He would often do the opposite, just to spite me, to punish me for daring to ask. I learned not to ask him for anything."

Sara nodded. "And you had to have great patience to put up with that, didn't you?"

Rachel nodded, trying not to break into tears again.

"And now, your patience has run out. When you ask your students to do something, you expect them to do it, to show you respect as any teacher has a right to expect. Don't think of it as losing patience with your students. Think of it as gaining confidence in yourself."

"But the students..." Rachel tried again. "What do I do about the students?"

"You will figure it out. It may take some time. You are navigating a new way of life. Give yourself time. But you will figure it out."

That night, Rachel woke up in tears. "Why?" she wondered aloud, until the memory of her dream slowly came back. She couldn't remember the details of it, but she did remember one thing—she had dreamed about her mom. Not the way her mom was when she'd passed away five years ago, just after Rachel had lost her baby. Not the way she was when Rachel was a teenager and had to take care of her. But the way she had been before Tim was born, before their dad left, before the depression had taken over her life. Then, she had been filled with joy and compassion for everyone. She always went out of her way to be friendly. Especially to those that really needed it—anyone with a physical disability and anyone who was a little bit odd, different, the underdog. Anyone, basically, that she knew needed some extra support in life.

Sometimes, Rachel wondered what made her mom care so much about helping others. It was almost like it was her life's mission. Later, when her mom fell into the depression, when she told Rachel things she never should have told someone of her age, Rachel understood her reason. It *was* her life mission, because of the pain she had dealt with for so long.

Her mom had been conceived during the Vietnam War, when Rachel's grandpa was visiting her grandma while he was home on shore leave. The two married soon after that—soon enough to avoid too much speculation. But there was never, really, any love between them. They had no love, either, to share with their daughter. It was a serious house that she grew up in. She used to dream that, just once, someone would smile at her. Which was why, when she got older, she always went out of her way to smile at others.

But it wasn't until her mom got pregnant with Tim—even though her dad had been gone for several weeks on a business trip—that Rachel's mom started to remember more about her early childhood and things that she had repressed for years: about her dad (Rachel's grandpa) and his late night visits into her room.

Rachel never asked her mom about how Tim was conceived or who his real dad was. She knew that her dad's best friend had come over to visit one night when her dad was gone on his trip. She'd heard some yelling that night, when she was in bed, but had been afraid to leave her room. And she knew that, when her father learned about the pregnancy, he left. Mom was never the same.

Rachel cried now, alone in her tiny cabin, for the mother she once knew, for what she must have gone through.

And for her own guilty feelings. Why hadn't she left her room that night? If she had just gone out there, perhaps she could have stopped...whatever had happened. And then, Mom would have stayed Mom and Dad would have stayed with her and everything would have been fine.

"It's not your fault," Rachel told herself, not for the first time. "You were a child. You were scared. You couldn't have been expected to protect your mother. You didn't even know what was happening. Besides," her mind added, "If you had gone out there, you probably wouldn't have Tim in your life now."

Rachel got out of bed, threw her coat over her pajamas, slipped on her shoes, and stepped outside. It was a clear night. The stars were out, as well as the full moon. She crossed the street and walked down the wooden stairs that led to the lakeshore. "Hello, Lake," she said, reaching down to touch its waters. "I am very glad to have you so close. Especially tonight."

Then she stood there for a while, just watching the moonlight sparkle and dance on the waves. Feeling the wind blowing on her face. And listening to the silence that can only be heard at two a.m. in the middle of nowhere.

I watched over her, again, that night. If I had arms, I would have reached out and held her as she struggled to deal with the

hard memories of her childhood. Instead, I let my beams dance on the water to cheer her up. And I worked on my plan to bring them together again, to help her find the arms that would hold her when she needed to cry.

Chapter 3

Rachel found a good deal on an old laptop at the second-hand store one day. She had always wanted to have a laptop, something she could write on, but Frank had always ridiculed the idea. "We have our home computer," he would say. "It works for everything we need it for. You can do your lesson plans on it. You can even check your work emails on it. What do you need a laptop for? It's just a waste of money, if you ask me." She didn't need a laptop, of course. The home computer did everything she needed. But she wanted one, all the same.

When she was younger, she used to dream of becoming an author. She wrote many stories as a young girl, and then poetry when she was a teenager. But by the time she got to college, the only thing she had time to write were term papers. And with Frank, she found that she couldn't write anything at all. What if he found it and read it? (And he always found what she didn't want him to find.) He would tell her how bad it was. In fact, she could hear his criticism before she even put a single word onto the page. And that fear kept her from writing anything at all.

But now, perhaps...

She got home and set the laptop up on her sewing machine. She had no Internet service (other than the data service on her cell phone) but that was okay. This computer wasn't for surfing the net. This computer was for writing on.

The computer fired up and she opened a word processing document.

Dear Diary, she typed, laughing good-naturedly at herself. It was, perhaps, a little immature to be writing to a diary at her age, but she hadn't written in so long. It was a place to start.

Where do I begin? she typed. *I left Frank back in August. It's October now and...*

Rachel heard the familiar "Ding!" at the end of the line and automatically reached for the carriage return.

She wasn't looking at her laptop anymore. Instead, she found she was sitting in front of a black, metal, Underwood Standard Portable Typewriter. The keys clacked and her hands—were they her hands?—quickly typed.

Dear Jebediah,

While I have enjoyed our acquaintance, I am afraid that I have to ask you to discontinue your attentions to me. As you know, as a schoolteacher, I am not allowed to keep company with any man that is not either my father or my brother. Your attentions, although pleasant, could have serious repercussions on my career, and I am afraid I just cannot risk it at this time. I appreciate your understanding on this matter.

Sincerely,
Annie

She finished typing this quickly, pulled it from the typewriter and signed it with her quill pen, before breaking into tears. She didn't want to write the letter. She didn't want to send Jebediah from her life. He was the first person who had ever made her feel special. He had been kind to her and listened to her, that day when things had gone so bad at school, the day she had almost been forced to give young Johnny Thomson a whipping.

She didn't want to, but he had cut off Mirabelle's braid, right near her head! What was she supposed to do? She had sent him home early, with a warning that she might have to have a talk with his pa later that day. But she was afraid to do that, too. If she didn't give Johnny a whipping, she was afraid that his pa would.

When Jebediah had stopped by just after school was out, to see if there was enough firewood for the woodstove, Annie had fallen to pieces in front of him. She couldn't help it—it had been such a hard day and she had been holding her emotions in for so long.

Jebediah wasn't put off by her outburst. It didn't even seem to make him uncomfortable. He just waited patiently until she had calmed down enough to tell him what was wrong. Then he listened quietly as she explained the whole situation.

"What do I do?" Annie had asked him at last.

"Well," said Jebediah. "As I see it, Johnny did something wrong, no doubt about it. And he deserves a punishment for what he did. Either you can give it to him or his pa will, but I'm thinking you might be a little bit more tender with what you dole out."

"But I don't want to whip him," Annie said again. "I mean, I know I'm supposed to, when the children get out of line. But..."

"But you don't want to hurt any of them," Jebediah supplied for her and she nodded. Jebediah thought for a moment, then looked at the dwindling stack of firewood outside the schoolhouse door. "Johnny is how old now? Twelve?"

"Thirteen," Annie replied.

Jebediah nodded. "Plenty old enough, then. Tomorrow, have him stay after school and he can help me chop some firewood. Perhaps he will be more respectful of this school—and everyone in it—when he's helped to take care of it."

So Johnny had stayed after school the next day with Jebediah, working well into the evening, filling the rack of firewood. If they talked at all while they were working, Annie never found out what they said. But she didn't have any trouble with Johnny misbehaving from then on. Or his twin brother, for that matter.

After that, Jebediah stopped by the school at least once a week, to see how Annie was getting along. She loved those times with him, and she hated the thought of ending them now. But she also knew what would happen if she let them go on any longer. She knew how people would talk. And if she lost her job as a teacher, then where would she go? Her own pa had made it quite clear, when she left for this job, that she wasn't to come back. He had his hands full with the farm and the other children and it was high time Annie made a life for herself, one way or another. If she wasn't going to get married right out of school, like her older sister did, well then she'd better be finding a way to support herself somehow. He wasn't mean—her pa—that was just the way things were. Annie had two choices. She could get married or she could become a teacher. And Annie was more interested in taking care of other people's children than in having her own, at least for now. Maybe someday things would be different. If she met the right man...

"Maybe Jebediah is the right man," she said aloud, glad she was alone in her room, where there was no one around to hear her. "Maybe," she sighed, but she didn't reckon that he was ready for his own children yet, either. He worked in the lumber mill and, from what Annie learned when she had asked around a bit, he was a good worker. But he was young and probably not ready to think about getting a wife yet. And Annie couldn't risk losing her income in the meantime.

"I have to do what I have to do," she told herself, folding the letter she'd typed and putting it into an envelope before sealing it and writing his name on the outside. She would give it to his boss to give to him. She couldn't face giving it to him herself.

Rachel came out of the trance slowly this time, as if waking from a dream. But it didn't feel like a dream. It felt so real to her. The typewriter. The tears. And Annie's thoughts. How had she known what Annie was thinking? How was she able to remember what Annie was remembering? And why was this happening?

When Annie walked home from school the next day, she swung by the lumber mill and left the letter with Jebediah's boss. After that, she didn't think about it at all. She didn't think about it as she did her chores that evening. She didn't think about it as she collected the eggs or as she milked the cow, part of her responsibilities for being allowed to board at the Wallace's place. And she definitely didn't think about it as she sat alone in her room, reading through the speeches that the fifth reader students had written. And she wasn't thinking about it at all, in fact, when there came a loud knock on the door.

She heard Mr. Wallace answer it and talk to the person at the door. She heard him say, "No, I'm sorry, she can't talk right now. It's too late." At that point, she knew who was there and whom he wanted to talk to. And she couldn't wait any longer. She came down the stairs. "I know I'm not suppose to talk to a man right now. I know it's too late. But couldn't I talk to him for just a minute? It's something very important to do with the school," Annie added, to try to cover up the truth of the matter.

"Please, sir," Jebediah added. "If you don't mind. It is very important."

"Well," said Mr. Wallace in a gruff tone. "I suppose you could sit here and talk to her for a moment, as long as I am right here too, of course."

Annie tried hard not to let out a sigh. How would they talk about anything with Mr. Wallace sitting right there?

But then Jebediah smoothed it over. "It's actually something for an upcoming event at the school. It's a secret right now. I don't want anybody to know about it yet. Would you mind if we just walked outside the window there. Right by the window, so you could keep an eye on us the whole time. It's just that I do need to talk to her in private, if you don't mind."

Mr. Wallace didn't look happy, but he nodded his head. "Very well, for the school. But I will be keeping an eye on you through the window."

"Of course," Jebediah said. "And thank you, sir!"

So Annie and Jebediah walked outside.

It was a beautiful moonlit night, the perfect sort of night for walking with your beau.

Except Jebediah is not my beau! Annie reminded herself silently. *He can't be. It's too big of a risk. I could lose too much!* she scolded herself.

"I mean to be your beau," Jebediah said aloud. "I read through your letter and I understand your concern. But I don't care about all that. You are different from any girl I've ever met and...well, I mean to make you my wife. If you'll have me."

"Jebediah Jones, are you proposing to me?" Annie asked.

"Well now, I reckon I am. Miss Annie, will you marry me?"

Annie nodded excitedly. "Yes, oh yes, I'd love to," she said, but then reality set in. "But how? I mean, where will we live? I can't really move into the boarding house with you and if I marry you, I can't keep teaching, and..."

"I'll find a way," Jebediah assured her. "I'll work odd jobs. I'll save every penny I make until I can buy us some land of our own, and then..."

"And then we can be together," Annie completed his thought. "But until then, I can't lose my job. You know that. I can't be seen with you. If I can keep working, I can save, too. Not much, because they don't pay me very much, since I am a woman, but I'll save what I can. In the meantime, we have to keep this all a secret."

Jebediah stopped walking and took Annie's hands in his. "We will be together," he assured her. "We were meant to be together, don't you feel it? It will work out."

Annie glanced away, suddenly uncomfortable by the intensity. When she did, she saw Mr. Wallace's face peering through the window, scowling. "I'd better go in," she told Jebediah, "before Mr. Wallace gets too upset. Or suspicious." Then, without even thinking about it, Annie added, "I wish we could just get into a car and drive away from all this."

Jebediah looked at her strangely. "Car? You mean a motorcar? Well, I wish I could afford such things, but if I had enough money for a motorcar, I would spend it to buy a place of our own."

Annie nodded in agreement, trying to cover up her own surprise at what she had said. *Why had she mentioned a motorcar?*

Once a month, the school Rachel worked for—which was a school that embraced and shared the culture of the

Anishinabe people, the Native Americans that lived in the U.P.—had what they called an opening celebration. Each opening was based on one of the Grandfather Teachings, which included wisdom, love, respect, bravery, honesty, humility, and truth.

Although she was not native herself, Rachel loved learning about Anishinabe culture and people. It felt almost as natural, as "comfortable" to her as her antiques did.

At the end of the ceremony, several of the boys sat around the school's drum, to play and sing in the traditional way of their people. Rachel had been told ahead of time that it was a sacred moment for their culture and that she should stand and show respect for the drum when it was played. She didn't need to be told. As soon as the drum started, Rachel knew in her heart that it was a sacred moment. She felt that the ancestors—hers as well as theirs—were close beside her. She closed her eyes, to better feel the power of the music.

When she opened them up again, she was no longer standing in the gym at her school. She was standing under the stars, under a full moon. There was a large bonfire in front of her and several wigwams behind, some covered with the traditional birch bark, some covered with tar paper or cloth. There was a drum playing, men were singing in a high-pitched wail, and men and women were dancing in a circle to the sound.

Then Jebediah walked up to her. "What do you think, Annie?" he asked. "I told you it was amazing."

"But how did you convince them to let us be here?" Annie asked, thinking about how they had snuck out of town, walking deep into the forest to find the Indian camp. "I thought they didn't much like outsiders."

"They like outsiders just fine," Jebediah explained, "when they know they can trust them. I work with some of these guys at the mill. I treat them like I would treat anyone else, but many people don't. Many whites have hurt the Indians over the years. Some have even tried to change them. Did you know, in some places not too far from here, they actually take the Indian kids away from their families and send them to boarding schools to try to make them more 'white'?"

"That is awful!" Annie replied. "Why would they do that?"

"Lots of reasons. Partly, it's an excuse to take away their lands. But it's more than that. They don't trust the Indian's ways. They don't understand..." Jebediah searched for the word, "this," he finally said, waving his hand at the fire, the drum, the dancers. "This is all strange to them. And a lot of people are afraid of what they don't understand."

"But how can they not understand?" Annie wondered out loud. "This is beautiful. And so spiritual. And so... true," Annie concluded at last, after struggling to find just the right word.

"Many people wouldn't understand it," Jebediah re-stated. "But I knew you would. That's why I convinced them to let me bring you here."

Annie felt warm inside, a warmth that was not created by her proximity to the fire. "Thank you," she whispered to Jebediah. "Thank you."

Things were going just fine for Rachel in her remote cabin. She was learning how to properly damper the fire so that the heat would last all night. (Actually, she learned a secret—if she got up once in the night to use the bathroom and added another log to the fire at that time, the cabin was still warm when she got up in the morning.)

She was enjoying life without easy access to the internet. She even found that she liked her long drives into town—it gave her plenty of think time. She was glad that she had chosen the "impractical" cabin after all.

Until the first storm of winter hit, a week before Thanksgiving.

It wasn't as if Rachel didn't know how to deal with snow. When she was living downstate with Frank, she had learned to shovel the driveway—if she wanted to get to work, she had to. Frank refused to bother with it until it was time for him to leave for the bar. So she knew how to deal with snow—or so she thought.

But when she stepped outside the first morning after the storm and saw her truck buried up to the windows, she suddenly realized that she knew nothing about winter in the U.P. She grabbed for her snow shovel, but honestly didn't even know where to start. How long would it take to dig her truck out? And where would she even put all the snow she moved? She was about to go inside, to call into work and tell them she couldn't make it, when a familiar truck pulled up with a plow on the front.

James hopped out and smiled at Rachel. "I was thinking you might need some help," he replied to her questioning look. "I normally charge extra for snow removal services. But this once..."

Part of her wanted to tell this man to go away, that she could handle this on her own. But the truth of it, she realized, was that she really couldn't. She needed help and the Universe had sent James to help her and she could hardly refuse a gift from the Universe. So instead of sending him away, Rachel just smiled and said "Thank you."

"Give me your truck keys and go on inside where it's warm," James told her. "I'll have this done in no time."

Rachel, feeling a bit guilty, handed him her keys and went back inside—just in time to hear her cell phone go off. School had been cancelled for the day. A snow day. She didn't need to worry about getting to work after all.

She got a fresh pot of coffee brewing. Then she started to cook some breakfast. James might appreciate a nice, warm meal after he was done with his work out in the cold.

Every once in a while, she would peek out the window to see how he was doing. The plow he had was made of two parts, so that he could adjust it to look like an arrow, a scoop, or a straight line, leaning in either direction. Rachel didn't know anything about plowing snow, but she could tell that James knew exactly what he was doing. He used the arrow-shape to plow through the middle of the driveway, then angled the blade, (first one way and then the other) to direct the snow to either side.

"You'll want to make sure to park your truck closer to the road from now on, roughly where I have it parked now," he told her when he came in. "And you should get in the habit of backing into the drive. It'll make it much easier to get past the plow bank at the road if you're heading forward."

Rachel nodded, taking mental notes. Then she told him she'd made some breakfast if he wanted any. He was about to refuse, but then she mentioned that it was biscuits and gravy. "Well, if you insist," he said.

She didn't have a table yet, so they sat on the couch, which was now nicely covered by a pale green sheet.

"Biscuits and gravy is my ultimate comfort food," he explained as he ate. "When I was younger, and living on the road, it was the cheapest meal I could get. And very filling. But this is better than anything I ever had at those truck stop diners."

Rachel smiled, proud of her ability to cook. She had Frank to thank for that—he had made sure she learned how to cook for him. Of course, for him everything had to be just right. And there was only one way—his way—to make anything. Still, she had learned a lot.

James launched into one of his many stories of life on the road, back in his teens and twenties. One story led to another and then another. It was well past noon when Rachel stood up to add more wood to the fire. At the same time, James stood up too. They stood there for a moment, face to face in uncomfortable silence.

"I was just going to..." Rachel started, just as James said, "I really should go now. I'm sure a few of my neighbors will still need to be plowed."

"Yes, of course," Rachel replied. "I've kept you too long already. But I do really appreciate you digging me out," she added.

"If you'd like, I can do it anytime you need, for just twenty dollars. That's probably the best price you'll find around here. I hate to charge anything, but I need to cover the cost of my gas and maintenance. Although, I might be willing to work for biscuits and gravy from time to time," he added with a wink.

"Sounds like a deal," Rachel replied, trying hard to ignore the way her heart leapt at the thought of him coming back again.

As she watched James drive away, Rachel thought to

herself, "I guess there are some times when having a man around is not such a bad thing. You know, like when there is a bunch of snow that needs to be taken care of," she added, in case her mind started to think of something else. "Although," she added, "perhaps someday..."

I might have been on the other side of the world at that moment, but I heard her thoughts, all the same. And I smiled to myself. She had removed the first chink in her armor and I knew love would find a way in. I would make sure of that.

Chapter 4

As soon as she'd gotten her new cell phone, Rachel had hired a lawyer—a nice woman that she felt she could trust—who had drawn up a petition of divorce and had it served to Frank. Then she had to wait for his response to the petition, then she had to file a counter response to his response. Then there were the negotiations back and forth. Rachel had thought this would be a relatively easy process. After all, they didn't have kids. They didn't even really have many possessions, other than the house. It should have been a simple case of splitting the assets 50/50 and moving on.

But Rachel quickly learned that divorce was never a case of 50/50—at least not with a man like Frank. First, he refused the petition of divorce altogether, telling his lawyer to tell her lawyer that he would not divorce her and she couldn't make him. Once he finally agreed to the divorce—probably because he finally realized that she wasn't coming back—he went after everything. The house that Rachel had paid for from the inheritance she got when her mom died. Their small joint savings account. Her retirement account. Anything he could squeeze out of her.

Rachel's lawyer suggested that she just accept his offer and move on with her life. "But it's not fair!" Rachel replied. "I worked hard for ten years, while he drank himself out of one job after another. He's not going to walk away with all the assets I have left," she told the lawyer. "I'm taking him to court. Surely the judge will see through all of his lies." If her lawyer thought otherwise, she never said so. She just worked with Rachel to prepare their statement for their day in court.

"Do you have anything that will help prove that he was an alcoholic and that this kept him from keeping a job?" she asked Rachel. "Records of sick days taken? Notifications of termination of employment? Anything?"

Rachel shook her head. "No, I didn't think to keep anything like that," she admitted.

"Any hospital records of him hurting you?" she asked next.

Rachel shook her head again. "The only time I actually went to the hospital was the time I fell down the stairs. And there's no way to prove that wasn't just an accident. I mean, maybe it was all an accident," Rachel added, the I'm-away-from-him-now-so-it-doesn't-seem-as-bad amnesia taking hold. "Either way, I don't want to bring any of that up. There's no need to drag up old dirt."

Again, if Rachel's lawyer thought differently, she didn't say anything.

On December first, Rachel drove back downstate for her court hearing. Her brother, Tim, drove over four hundred miles to be with her that day, so she wouldn't have to face it alone. She wasn't sure if she would ever be able to tell him just how much that meant to her.

They got to the courthouse early. As they were waiting in the entranceway for their turn, Rachel caught sight of Frank for the first time since she had left him. She was suddenly overcome with a fear she hadn't felt in months. She gripped Tim's hand tightly, so thankful that he was there. "If Tim wasn't here," she admitted silently to herself, "I might have run over there and begged him to take me back, just out of the fear of what he would do if I didn't."

And then, finally, it was their turn to go in.

Although Rachel had wanted to keep things on a respectful level, Frank had no such qualms. He brought up every bit of dirt he could on her, even digging out the story of her "on-line affair."

It had happened just after her mother died and only months since the loss of her baby.... She was dealing with this double grief and also with feeling guilty that she had put her mom into a nursing home. So she turned to an online support group to help her through it. There was one man, in particular, that she really connected with, as they chatted of their mixed feelings about their parents.

Rachel had felt like she was finally being understood. But when the conversation turned from an atmosphere of support to that of romance, Rachel panicked. She cut the conversation off immediately. Dropped out of the group. Blocked him from all communication with her. And then told Frank.

She thought he'd be supportive. She thought he would see how, by stopping things, she showed her loyalty. She wanted to be totally honest with him. She had no idea how he would take everything and twist it. She was a slut for flirting with another guy. She clearly didn't really love Frank anymore. She just did it in order to hurt him. She was the evil bitch he always knew that she was.

After five years, the wound from that mistake had healed—or so Rachel thought. Now it was being brought up again, for the whole courtroom to hear, with all of its former sting and shame. Rachel wanted to break down right there and cry, but she knew she couldn't. She had to hold it together. She had to explain her side of things. She had to make the judge see the truth.

But when it was her turn on the witness stand, things did not go as planned. Her lawyer asked the questions they had prepared and all was fine. Then Frank's lawyer got his turn.

"Did you, Rachel Smith, leave your husband on August twentieth of this year?"

Rachel nodded her head.

"I'm sorry," the lawyer responded, "I can't hear you. Can you please say your answer so the court stenographer can record it?"

"Yes, I did," Rachel replied.

"And did you give him any warning ahead of time that you were going to leave?"

Rachel shook her head. "No," she said aloud. "But I didn't because I was afraid..."

"Just answer the question," the lawyer interrupted her. "Did you know before that day that you were planning to leave him?" he asked next.

"Yes," Rachel mumbled.

"Yes, you did, didn't you? Because you already had a job offer waiting for you. Right? A job offer you knew about since early July, is that true?"

"Yes."

"But you didn't bother to tell your husband about your plans?"

"No."

"And was that new job over 300 miles away from your husband?" he asked Rachel.

"Yes," Rachel answered, wondering what the lawyer was getting at.

"And that means it was also over 300 miles away from your home, right? So you obviously weren't planning on commuting to work, were you?"

"I...uh...no..." Rachel was confused. She felt like she

was being backed into a corner but she wasn't quite sure how.

"That house is no good to you with your new job, isn't that right?"

"Um, I guess."

"So you had no intention of keeping that house, did you? You didn't want it. You had no use for it. You left it for my client. Right?"

"Well, I left, but..."

"You left the house, with my client still living in it, and moved over 300 miles away. Is that correct? And you just agreed that you weren't planning on commuting to work and that the house was of 'no good to you.' But that house is of value to my client. In the past four months, he has lived there, paid the bills, taken care of the maintenance and upkeep, all while you would have just left it standing empty. You clearly don't care about the house but my client does." It wasn't a question and Rachel didn't know what she could have said, anyway. Then the lawyer turned to the judge. "I rest, your honor."

In the end, Frank took everything—he got the house, he got the savings account, he got half of her retirement account. The other half had to be liquidated, even though it incurred penalties for early withdrawal, so Rachel could pay off her lawyer. She left the courtroom that day with only one thing—her freedom. And it was worth every penny!

After she got through her divorce proceedings, the next thing Rachel had to get through was Christmas. It should have been easy. After all, for the first time ever, Rachel had no responsibilities. She didn't have anyone she had to buy presents for, except maybe a little something for Tim now that he was back in her life. She didn't have to worry about cooking or baking or shopping or really any of the things that added to the holiday madness. She could just relax and enjoy the season at her own pace.

But Rachel found that she couldn't relax. She kept feeling like she should be doing something and felt restless and guilty and sad. Christmas had always been a big deal to her. Ever since Tim was a baby, Rachel had been playing Santa to him—she knew her mother wasn't going to and she didn't want Tim to go without. Even long after he must have stopped believing the story, they still played out their parts, right up until he left for college. And then, Rachel had Frank to spoil each Christmas. She would take every little bit of money they had left by the end of the year, everything she had been able to save, and showered him with gifts. If she gave him enough, he would be happy. If she bought him just the right thing, he would finally realize how much she loved him. And he would love himself, and...

Now, without someone to buy presents for, Rachel felt lost. It was a good thing she didn't have to buy a bunch of presents, because she didn't have much money to spare, anyway. But it just didn't feel right.

Finally, Rachel decided to talk to Sara, the school counselor, about it. Maybe she could help her learn to relax a little and let go.

"I want to buy Christmas presents, but I don't have anyone to buy for and I really don't have any money to spend and I should just let it go and relax but I can't seem to and…"

Sara smiled gently. "The first Christmas—or any holiday—after a loss is always difficult. And make no mistake about it, Rachel. You have gone through a loss. A welcome one and one that will be so much better for your soul in the long run, but it is still a loss. It's a loss of who you were with him. And you need to grieve for that."

Rachel nodded, but inside wondered if she could handle much more grieving. Couldn't she just get on with her life, already?

Sara continued. "One thing that helps is to create some new traditions. So I'm going to give you some homework," she said with a smile. "Two assignments, actually. Here's the first—I want you to create a new tradition with somebody else. Bake cookies or go sledding or caroling or shop 'til you drop. But you have to do it with someone else—some reflective time is good, but sitting at home by yourself all day isn't good for you."

"I'll try," Rachel replied, not sure who she could find to do anything with. She was friendly with the other teachers, but they all seemed to have their own lives and she didn't want to bother them.

"That's your first assignment," Sara told her, interrupting her thoughts. "Here is your second: this year, I want you to buy presents for the most important person in your life—you. I know you don't have much money, but go to the thrift shops, look on clearance racks, be creative. When you wake up Christmas morning, I want you to have presents wrapped and waiting under the tree."

Rachel laughed at the idea.

"I'm serious," Sara told her. "Give yourself the kind of Christmas you always wanted—the kind of Christmas you always gave to someone else. It's your turn."

Rachel stood up and gave Sara a bit of a salute. "Aye, aye, captain!" she said and smiled. "I'll do my best."

So Rachel spent the rest of the month bargain shopping. She went to thrift shops and resale stores. She shopped the clearance racks and on-line. Before too long, she had a whole pile of presents under her tree—and she had a tree, which she also picked up for a deal at the resale store, along with stockings to hang on the fireplace and some garland for around the windows. At first, she felt silly wrapping presents for herself, but the festive way they looked under the tree made it totally worth it.

As it turned out, buying presents for herself was the easy part. The harder part for Rachel was starting a new tradition with someone else. She couldn't think of what to do and even worse, she had no idea who to invite to do it with her.

That is, until the answer to both questions walked into her cabin. She was in the kitchen area baking sugar cookies—because you just have to have cookies at Christmastime. She was playing her music on high and singing along, which is why she didn't realize someone had come in until she looked up and saw James right next to her. She almost jumped out of her skin.

"Sorry, I..." James tried to scream over the music. Rachel held up a finger to indicate to wait, then fumbled around for the "off" button on her old CD player. Once the music stopped, James tried again. "I'm sorry," he said. "I didn't mean to scare you. I tried knocking, but I didn't get an answer and I could tell someone was home, so..." He didn't say "Your music was blasting so loud I knew you were here," but it was implied.

Rachel smiled at being caught at her own foolishness. But she didn't feel embarrassed by it.

"I came to see if you wanted to go snowshoeing with me," James explained. "But it looks like you're busy, so I'll let you be."

Rachel's eyes lit up. "Snowshoeing? I've never been snowshoeing before. I'd love to. Let me just…" Rachel looked around, at the flour-covered kitchen counter and the bowl half-filled with ingredients.

James smiled. "You have the recipe here?" James asked, pointing at the recipe card half-covered in flour. "I'll tell you what. I'll finish adding everything while you get ready. Then the dough can chill and we can cook it when we get back."

Rachel smiled, impressed with how quickly James had taken in the situation and come up with a solution. And impressed that he was willing to help her cook. "Are you making a single batch or a double?" James asked, further impressing her.

"A double batch," she confirmed. "I've already put in the flour, salt, and baking soda. It still needs everything else."

"Got it," James replied. "You go get yourself ready."

So Rachel went into the small bedroom to get ready for their excursion. That's when she realized her next problem—what was she going to wear? She had a winter coat, of course, but she didn't have snow pants or winter boots. "I am really unprepared for this life," she mumbled to herself as she tried to come up with a solution.

When she finally emerged from the bedroom, she had on two pairs of jeans—"It's a good thing I kept that pair that was too big on me," Rachel thought to herself—and two pairs of socks, in addition to a flannel shirt. She put on her sneakers, her winter coat and gloves, and threw a scarf around her neck. She didn't have a hat, either.

James saw her getting ready and smiled as he put the completed cookie dough in the fridge. She clearly didn't have the right equipment for the weather, but she was trying. She hadn't used that as an excuse not to go. He admired that about her.

He also quickly noted to himself that the walk shouldn't last too long—she was going to be freezing in no time. He had the feeling this girl wasn't going to complain if she got too cold—she'd just keep going out of pure stubbornness. It was up to him to stop when she needed him to.

He drove them to a nearby hiking trail and showed her how to strap the metal and rubber snowshoes on. "Just follow me and try to stay close," he told her by way of instruction. "Oh, and I hope you don't mind, but I am packing," he said, patting the glock at his side, "just in case we run into any wolves or bears. I won't hurt them if I don't have to," he explained, "but it's good to be prepared, just in case. I hope that doesn't make you too uncomfortable."

"Of course not," Rachel replied automatically, and then thought about it. *Did it make her uncomfortable?* As a general rule, she didn't like guns. Her uncle had been killed in the Gulf War and after that, her mother would never let her or Tim play with guns, even toy ones. But this was different. It was clear that James didn't see this as a play-thing, but necessary equipment for walking in the woods in a remote area of the Upper Peninsula of Michigan, where things like bear encounters could actually happen. She found that she felt a bit more comfortable knowing he had his gun by his side.

James led the way and Rachel followed behind him, doing her best to keep up with his longer strides. Since it was impossible to walk side by side, it was also impossible to talk as they walked. At first, this made Rachel uncomfortable. "What was James thinking?" she wondered. "Why had he invited me to go with him? Does he regret it now? Does he think I'm too slow? Does he..." Rachel stopped the thought process right there, scolding herself for "thinking too much." "He invited me because he wanted me to join him," she reminded herself. "And he hasn't turned around and taken me back yet, so that's a good sign." After that, she was able to let go of her worries and just enjoy the moment.

It was beautiful. The sun was out, making millions of shiny diamonds on the crusted snow. Her snowshoes made a gentle crunching sound with each step she took. From somewhere, she heard the tweeting of a bird. "What type of bird," she wondered, "would still be here in the winter?" Then she spotted the little chickadee on a branch in the tree in front of her and smiled.

When she looked down at her feet again, her snowshoes

had changed. They were no longer metal with a black rubber skin covering them. Now, they were made of a bent wood, interlaced in an intricate pattern with sinew. Rachel knew she was no longer herself anymore—she was Annie.

"Wait up, Jeb!" she called out. "My legs aren't as long as yours."

Jebediah turned around and looked at Annie, her face flushed from the cold winter wind and the exercise. "Come on," he urged her. "I want to show you something."

Annie followed as quickly as she could, turning around a corner just after Jebediah did. And there, Annie saw the most beautiful thing she had ever seen—a small waterfall. At the top, the ice formed a crust, but under that crust, the water still flowed as quickly as ever. But what made it so beautiful was the way the sunlight sparkled on the water. Every little reflection seemed to be dancing, just like Annie's heart seemed to dance every time Jebediah was near.

He looked back to see Annie's reaction. "I love the way your face lights up when you see something pretty," he told her with a smile. "For the rest of your life, I hope I can always show you beautiful things."

As they continued on their way, Annie was smiling even more. She loved the idea of spending the rest of her life with Jebediah. She just hoped things worked out like they'd planned. So far, they had found ways to be together, without anyone suspecting anything. She had snuck out of the farm house, like a young girl, when Jebediah had invited her to go to the Indian ceremony. Even to be with him now, she had to tell Mr. Wallace that she was going on a walk, alone, to help "clear her head so she could focus on planning her lessons." She knew that they couldn't keep things secret forever. And once people knew about the two of them, that would be the end of her job.

Which would be sad, not just because she still needed the money but because she was really enjoying being a teacher, now that the Johnson twins were under control. The kids seemed to be learning well. They were getting ready for a presentation night for the community soon. Annie had thought it up when she realized that they really did need some kind of "surprise at school" like they had told Mr. Wallace about. But she was glad she did, because the kids were really getting excited about it. Every student had to present something, but they got to choose what they wanted to present. Some of them were reciting poems. A few of the older girls were going to put on a play. Even the younger ones were going to be singing "The A.B.C., a German Air with Variations for the Flute with an Easy Accompaniment for the Piano Forte."

Annie, lost in her own thoughts, was suddenly brought back to reality by the sound of a low grunting behind her. She slowly turned her head and found herself eye to eye with a large black bear. It must have been hiding under the fallen log they had just walked by.

She stood there, frozen for a moment as they each read the others' soul. Then she heard a whir and a thwack. In an instant, a hatchet was buried deep in the bark of a tree next to the bear. Annie glanced at Jebediah and he held another hatchet in his hand, poised to throw.

The bear also looked at him for a minute, as if trying to decide if he was worth the bother. Then it shook its shaggy head, turned around, and lumbered off in the other direction.

As soon as it was completely out of sight, Annie ran as fast as her snowshoes would allow and threw herself at Jebediah, almost knocking them both down in the process.

"Thank you," she said over and over, "Thank you for saving me and thank you for not hurting that bear. It didn't want to hurt me. I could see that in its eyes. It just wasn't expecting to see anyone here, by its home, this late in the winter and..."

As Annie rambled on, Jebediah held her close, trying to calm his own quickly-beating heart. This wasn't his first encounter with a bear out in these woods, of course. But this was different. This time, it was his Annie that was in danger. This time, he had more to lose than just his life, and he couldn't stand the thought of that!

"Are you doing okay?" James asked Rachel, bringing her back to the present. "You're not too cold are you?"

Rachel shook her head, despite the numbness she was

feeling in her fingers and toes. "Tomorrow," she silently told herself, "I will go into town and find some proper winter clothes."

James saw her shake her head and smile, but he also saw her body shiver slightly. It was time to go back.

"You might be fine," he told her, "but I'm getting a bit chilly. What do you say we go back and finish making those cookies?"

"Perfect," Rachel agreed, trying not to sound too excited.

When they got back to the cabin and James was helping Rachel to unstrap her snowshoes, he noticed that her woodpile was almost out. He thought about offering to refill it for her, but stopped himself. Although he felt a strong desire to help take care of this woman, he also sensed that she needed to feel that she could take care of herself.

"It looks like you'll be needing more firewood soon," he noted. "I can give you the number for a guy who sells it by the truckload. You'll want him to dump it right over there," he pointed, "so it's easy to get to but doesn't block your way. It will be cut to stove-lengths, but you'll have to split it yourself. However, there is a splitting maul along with a sledge and wedge by the back door for you to use."

"Sounds good," Rachel replied. "Thank you."

James chuckled silently to himself. "She has no idea what I'm talking about," he thought to himself, "but she's not going to admit it. Too proud, I guess. Or too insecure. Either way, I just hope she doesn't hurt herself trying to figure it out."

Rachel silently vowed to google "sledge," "wedge," and "splitting maul" as soon as James left.

"So, shall we finish up those cookies?" James asked. "I'd hate to leave here today without getting to try at least one."

Rachel smiled and led him inside. "Make yourself at home," she told him as she went to her room to strip off the two pairs of very wet, very heavy jeans. She didn't have any other jeans to put on, so she finally just slipped on a long brown skirt, something she normally wore for school. It looked a bit silly with the flannel shirt, perhaps, but she didn't have many options.

When she came out again, James was already at work on the cookies. He had covered the counter with flour and was rolling out the first batch of dough. Rachel smiled to herself, seeing him using her mom's old rolling pin and then reaching for the tin of metal cookie cutters that had once been her grandmother's. These had been some of the things that Rachel had made sure to bring when she left Frank.

Then she took a deep breath, working up the courage to step outside her comfort zone. "So, um…" Rachel tried, as she joined him in cutting out cookie shapes. "I mean, I was wondering if…" she tried again.

James looked at her expectantly, but didn't say anything.

"I don't know if you have anyone to spend Christmas

with but, if not, I mean, I don't have anyone and, well, it might be nice if you wanted to come over."

James smiled at her, thinking about how cute she looked when she blushed. "That would be nice," he agreed. Normally he went downstate to visit his dad on Christmas, but he didn't think he should bring that up right now—not after how hard it was for her to even ask him. He could make a road trip some other time. He had a feeling that, if he told him about the woman he was spending Christmas with, his dad would understand.

The woman, he thought, repeating the words in his head. In some ways, Rachel was like a delightful little girl, full of both wonder and determination. But in other ways, she was very much a woman, he thought, noticing how the skirt she was wearing accented her hips nicely. And as she turned and leaned over to put the cookies in the oven... Well, he wasn't thinking of her as a little girl, that was for sure.

As soon as James left—many hours later—Rachel called the guy he'd suggested about getting more firewood. Then she used the data plan on her phone to figure out what those words he'd used meant.

"Sledge: short for sledgehammer."

"Wedge: a piece of hard material with two faces meeting in a sharp angle, for splitting objects by applying a pounding or driving force, as from a hammer."

"Maul: to handle or use roughly; a heavy hammer, as for driving stakes or wedges."

"Oh," thought Rachel. "So they are things for splitting the wood. Got it." Then for extra good measure, she watched a few videos to see exactly how they were used. "There, I'm an expert now," she said to herself.

But when the guy came a few days later and dumped a big pile of wood in the yard, she discovered that she wasn't such an expert, after all. She put on her newly-bought snowsuit, which she had found at the second-hand store. It looked like it had come straight out of the 70s, and probably had, but it fit her well and would keep her warm. She hadn't yet found the perfect deal on boots, so her tennis shoes would have to do, even if they did end up getting soaking wet. But she did now also have a nice scarf, hat, and mitten combo to wear.

The mittens were the first things to come off. She couldn't hold the sledge with them; they were too slippery. The next problems she had were in getting the logs to stand up on end and then splitting them into smaller pieces. In the videos she'd watched, the guys just set the log down, tapped on the wedge to drive it into the wood, then they swung the sledgehammer down on the wedge and...TADA, perfectly split pieces.

It didn't go that smoothly for Rachel. The logs would

fall over. The wedge wouldn't stay in place. And if she could finally get that much to work, she would hold the sledgehammer over her shoulder then bring it down, only to miss the log completely. She tried again and again, with the same disastrous results. When she just barely avoided bringing the sledge down on her big toe, she decided it was time for a new approach.

She set the sledge and the wedge out of the way and grabbed the splitting maul, instead. The splitting maul was like a sledgehammer and a wedge that had been welded together. And it was lighter than the sledge. According to the videos Rachel had watched, it wasn't as powerful and didn't work as well on the really big logs. But if she could control it and maybe even hit the log from time to time, she'd be doing better than she had with the sledge.

The maul did prove to be much more suited for Rachel. With less weight to steady, she had more ability to control where it went. She hit the first log and felt the satisfying sensation of having it easily split into two smaller parts.

"It splits easier because of the cold," Rachel thought to herself. "The wood always splits easier when it's frozen." She nodded, as if agreeing with herself, then stopped in mid-swing. "How did I know that?" she wondered. They hadn't said that in any of the videos. And James hadn't mentioned it. It was just like she knew, somehow.

She started her swing again, but as she brought the

maul down, she was no longer Rachel, standing by her cabin. She was Annie, standing behind the barn at the Wallace farm. The one thing that hadn't changed was the stack of firewood in front of her.

Because of the long winters and short growing seasons, there were not a lot of farms in the area. Most people made a living from lumber—either chopping it down or cutting it into boards—or fishing. And there were the cranberry farms that seemed to do well in this location. But Mr. Wallace was determined to make a living here by farming. He had cows and chickens and grew hay, as well as potatoes, squash, and beans. He never got rich with his farm, but he was able to provide for his family.

Mr. Wallace had three boys that had survived until adulthood. He also had a young daughter—Sissy—who was now eight. But she had been sickly ever since she was born. When her mom had died during childbirth, folks had expected her to follow soon after. But she survived. Still, she wasn't strong enough to be much help around the farm. And when his grown sons left to go downstate for more opportunities, Mr. Wallace was forced to run the farm all by himself.

That is, until he agreed to provide room and board for the new school teacher. In the past, the teacher had been asked to move from house to house throughout the year. But Mr. Wallace had made the concession to have her stay at his farm year round, to "make it easier for her."

It hadn't taken Annie long to figure out the real reason he'd been willing to provide her food and a place to stay— she was expected to earn her keep. Today, that meant she was splitting wood.

"This had been easier," she thought, "during the heart of winter. When the wood was frozen, it split with much less work." But now spring was coming and the weather was warming up. This made Annie feel almost giddy inside, but it did make the job of chopping wood harder. Before long, she was sweating in her calico dress, even as the sun was getting low in the sky and the full moon was rising.

She stopped to wipe the sweat away and noticed someone walking through the field toward her. As he got closer, she could see clearly who it was: Jebediah.

"Now what if someone had seen you?" she scolded him as soon as he was near enough.

Jebediah just smiled at her. "There ain't no one about these parts," he told her, "except Mr. Wallace and little Sissy. Mr. Wallace is busy trying to dig up an old stump out by the southern corner of the property and will likely be there until it gets too dark to see. And Sissy fell asleep on the porch, reading a book."

Annie knew that Jebediah wouldn't be there unless it was safe. He was always very careful. She felt bad for scolding him.

"Besides," he continued. "I had to come see you. I

wanted to give you this." He handed her a small brown paper package.

She slowly opened it to discover a leather-bound book. When she opened it up, the pages were all blank.

"It's for you to write in," he explained. "For writing down your memories and thoughts. I know you have a lot to share, and I can't always be here to talk to. So I figured, when you can't talk to me..." Jebediah stopped talking, suddenly afraid of how Annie would react to the present. Maybe she wouldn't like it after all.

"I love it!" Annie said, flinging herself at him and wrapping her arms around him. He held her for a long while, feeling her heartbeat against his own chest. She finally pulled away slightly and their eyes met. And then their lips.

It was as if their love, which until this point had been expressed with words and tender looks, suddenly needed another way to express itself. Something more—something big enough to contain the depths of their feelings. Something as strong as the love that had taken over their whole bodies, their whole souls.

Annie pulled away enough to ask, shyly, "You said Sissy was asleep on the porch?"

Jebediah nodded. "And Mr. Wallace is off in the southern pasture..."

Annie took Jebediah by the hand, silently led him around the corner and into the barn, then to the ladder that led to the hayloft. She silently climbed it and he scrambled up behind her.

"Are you sure, Annie?" Jebediah asked.

Annie just nodded as she untied her skirt and let it fall to the floor, along with her petticoat. Then she unbuttoned her blouse and took that off, as well. Finally, she undid her corset. Then, dressed in only her chemise and bloomers, she laid herself down on the hay. Jebediah quickly slipped off his britches and shirt, down to his long underwear, and eased himself down gently on top of her. Their lips met again. Their hands fumbled over each others bodies, above their remaining clothing. Then reaching beneath the clothes to feel skin on skin. Jebediah's hand found its way to the opening between Annie's bloomers and felt the warmth of her within. He could wait no more. He unbuttoned his long johns and let himself out into the air. And then into her.

It was as if nothing else in the world existed in that moment, except the two of them, there in the hayloft, consumed in their love for each other. I watched over them, protecting them from afar, making sure that no one disturbed this magical moment. There were going to be some hard times, soon, for both of them. But for this brief time, nothing mattered but the two of them, together once again.

Chapter 5

Rachel came out of her trance this time feeling a bit guilty for "being there." It was obviously a private time between Annie and Jebediah. But she couldn't control when she had these images or how long she stayed in Annie's mind. "Why Annie?" Rachel wondered. "I mean, I wonder why it happens at all, but if it is going to happen, why do I always see through Annie's eyes? I wonder if she is me in a past lifetime or something?" Rachel laughed at this idea, but the more she thought about it, the more it seemed to make sense. Because she wasn't just seeing what Annie was seeing, she was feeling what Annie was feeling (yes, all of it, Rachel thought with a blush.) It was more like a memory than a vision.

And that latest memory had a big effect on Rachel over the course of the next few days. She caught herself smiling for no reason at all. And then feeling frustrated. And restless. And...It had been a while since she had left Frank, and even longer since they had "been together."

No matter where she was emotionally, her body was ready to be in a relationship again.

"Perhaps, when James comes over for Christmas…" Rachel allowed herself to think. "I mean, I am an adult woman. We are both adults and if… It doesn't have to be a big thing, right? Just take care of our needs and…"

Perhaps because of this, Christmas day turned out to be more stressful than it needed to be. In addition to all the presents she'd bought for herself, Rachel had gone back to the second-hand store to find some unique (and cheap) gifts for James, as well. But she had struggled with what to get him. "How well do I really know him?" she wondered, quickly followed by "Why did I ever invite him over?"

But the presents were bought and James was coming over and… Rachel tried her best not to worry about anything beyond that. If he liked his presents, great. If not, oh well, she had tried. And as far as anything else, well, she would just have to see how things went.

He did like her gifts—very thoughtful presents—including a matchbox truck just like his, complete with a tiny plow on the front, and an antique wooden box with delicate inlay. "How did she know how much I like well-crafted woodwork?" he wondered to himself. "Have I ever mentioned it to her?"

He was very happy with the gifts, but then quickly felt himself feeling unhappy. "Why had she given these things to you?" his doubt asked him. "What does she want from you? Is she going to try to come in and take over your life, the way they all do eventually?"

"Not this time," he told his doubts, and he instantly felt his walls build up.

Rachel felt the walls, but had no idea where they were coming from. They'd been having a nice time. He seemed to like his gifts. And so, as women tend to do, she decided that it must have been her fault, that she did something wrong. Maybe she'd said the wrong thing or smiled the wrong way or who knows what. But she felt like she had to make it right. So she smiled more. She reached out and touched his leg. She complimented him.

And then he, sensing that she wasn't acting "normal," decided that he must be right—she did want something from him. Why else would she be acting like this? "Not this time," he repeated in his head. "I'll get what I need from her, but I'm not going to let her get too close to me."

The night ended as Rachel had predicted, with them having sex, on the floor in front of the fire. But it was not what Rachel had dreamed it would be. Their bodies were close, but she felt further away from him than ever. She felt like she had in the later years with Frank—where each was doing what they had to, but there was no love involved.

James left soon after they were done, which was fine with Rachel. All she wanted to do was cry. And cry. And cry. Not just about what had happened that night, not just about the distance she'd felt from James, the rejection she'd felt from him, even as his body had said yes. All of that just reminded her of all the pain she had felt with Frank. About how often she had tried to reach him, tried to get him to love her as he had—or as he seemed to at least—in the beginning. It was almost like she had been a junkie, Rachel thought now, addicted to Frank's love. She needed it, to a point where nothing else mattered but trying to get it. And he withheld it from her. Or sometimes, she realized, he would give it to her, just a taste. Just enough to keep her addicted.

"Just like Mom would," she said aloud, before even thinking about it. But once she said it, she knew it was true. Most of the time, her mom was distant—caught up in her own world of depression and grief. But once in a while, she was really there for Rachel. She cared about how Rachel was doing. She wanted to hear what Rachel had to say. She made Rachel feel special. And it was because of those moments that Rachel could never really hate her or even stay mad at her for all she put her through. She loved her mom, understood what she was dealing with, and forgave her over and over again. Just like she forgave Frank, over and over again.

At that thought, Rachel started bawling once more.

After she calmed down again, Rachel decided that it was time to open her great-aunt's trunk. It wasn't a big trunk—maybe two feet by three feet. Easy enough to pick up and take with her when she left Frank. And valuable enough, in her mind, that she knew she had to keep it.

Inside, Rachel stored things that were attached to special memories from her life, including the best gift she had ever gotten for Christmas—a porcelain doll that she had always wanted and her mom had finally gotten for her when she was eight, because she was "now old enough to take proper care of it." The doll had a crack around its entire face, from when her dad had fixed it after she'd accidently dropped it on the sidewalk and the whole face had broken off. So it was special to her in two ways—because her mom trusted her enough to give it to her and because her dad had taken the time and effort to fix it for her.

There were other things in there, as well: some of the most special cards and letters she'd gotten over the years, a bubblegum cigar that her mom had passed out when Tim was born, and a friendship bracelet she'd gotten in third grade.

She also had the cards she'd given Frank during their marriage, and the ones he'd given her, too. Rachel read them now, even though it hurt to do so. In his cards, he was always so sweet. They were mostly apologies—saying he was sorry for whatever he had done and promising to do better in the future. Always ending by saying how much he loved her, how important she was to him, and how he would do anything to make her happy.

This brought on another whole round of crying. "I

loved him so much!" Rachel admitted to the air around her. "And he really seemed like he loved me too. At least, at times—when he wasn't drunk or trying to make me feel bad. He said he wanted to make me happy. And at times, he really did. He'd buy me flowers or chocolates or take me out to dinner and then..." Some memories were too precious to say aloud, even if there was no one else around to hear them. She cried again, grieving over the man he seemed to be when he was showing her he loved her, grieving over the man she thought he would one day become all the time. Because now, she was forced to face facts head-on. He wasn't that man, probably had never really been that man, and would never become that man now. She had let go of the man he really was over four months ago without any real trouble. It was much harder, now, to let go of the dream of who he could have been, if she had just tried harder, worked harder, loved him more. It was very hard to let that dream go, but she knew that, if she didn't, she would never truly be free of him.

When she finally calmed down again, when all of her tears were spent, she packed up the trunk. Then she put on her coat and stepped out into the cold winter's night.

She looked up at the full moon, one very much like the one that had shined down on her the night she drove away from Frank, and quietly said, "Thank you, whoever or whatever you are, for giving me the strength to get through this, for giving me the courage to try, and for giving me the ability to see the truth behind the role Frank tried to play. I realize now that he was never going to become the man I hoped he could be. I think I am ready to say goodbye to that dream forever."

I smiled down on her, on her words, on her intentions behind them, and on her heart, which I felt finally begin to melt. "You're welcome," I whispered back to her. Although she couldn't hear my words, of course, I knew she felt them, just the same.

Annie was glad that Jebediah had given her the journal to write in. Because now, she had a secret to write in it, something she hadn't told anybody about yet—not even Jeb. It had been several months since their time together in the hayloft. And in that time, she had not been visited by her "monthly sickness." But she had been feeling sick, every morning when she got up, for weeks. She hadn't told anybody, but she knew her body well enough to know the truth of the matter—she was pregnant.

She wrote in her journal, keeping the lettering small, with no margins, so as not to waste any of the precious paper.

Dear Diary,
    I've tried to deny the truth as long as I can, but I have to

face facts. I am going to have Jebediah's baby. The idea delights me, and terrifies me all at the same time. I am delighted at the thought of having his baby, the idea that our love for each other brought a new life into this world. Even the fear of childbirth doesn't diminish this joy. But the realities of our life does. I'm not sure how long I'll be able to hide this from everyone. And once they know the truth, what will they think of me? I am a teacher. I am unmarried. It will be a scandal. I will be labeled immoral. Or worse! I will surely lose my job and...oh, what am I going to do?

Annie couldn't write any more, because she was crying too hard. What was she going to do? She had tried to do the right thing, the proper thing, by telling Jebediah to stop seeing her. She knew it was what she "should" do. But even at the time, her heart had told her it was not what she needed to do. They belonged together—there was no doubt in her mind about that. But where? And how? That, she did not know.

The next morning, Rachel felt better. "Sometimes," she thought, "crying is just what is needed."

She hummed to herself as she prepared the morning fire, starting with cleaning out all the ashes from the night before. It seemed to be symbolic, in a way. Before she could start something new—something that could bring warmth to her life—she had to clear out the remains of what was left behind from the past. That, she realized, was what all the crying had been about the night before. She had been clearing away the ashes left over from her past life with Frank. She had thought that she was well over him, but sometimes, you can't totally deal with your emotions from an old relationship until you are in a new one. "Not," Rachel said aloud to the empty cabin, "that I need to be in a new relationship in order to get over my last one. At least, not in that way. But there is something about being with someone new that triggers some things I hadn't considered before. Still, why in the world did I have sex with James last night?"

Rachel thought about that as she got the new fire going and as she ate her breakfast. After that, she pulled out her laptop and started to write.

Dear Diary,

A lot has happened since last time I wrote to you—in fact, a lot has happened since yesterday. But the biggest one is that I slept with James. And I'm not quite sure why. I mean, yes, my body wanted it. And James seemed willing. But that doesn't explain why I let it happen. I mean, if it had been "a romantic joining of two souls into one," perhaps I could understand that. But it wasn't. It was—empty. Instead of two souls joining, it was like our souls weren't even there. Just two bodies going through the motions. I mean, it wasn't bad, but it sure didn't bring me closer to James. In fact, I feel further away from him than ever.

Rachel paused for a moment after writing that, thinking, dissecting that day to see if she could tell what went wrong—and when. James had seemed so distant. Not like he normally was. It had bothered her a lot. She felt him pull away from her, for whatever reason, and she had changed how she acted, too. She had done everything she could to pull him back to her. She had even...

I slept with James because I felt him pull away, she wrote on her laptop, only realizing it as she wrote it down. *I felt him withdraw from me and I panicked. I had to "get him back," at whatever the cost. I threw myself at him in a desperate effort to keep him from running.* She wrote that in a flurry, and then stopped to think about what she'd written. Why had she been so afraid of "losing" James, she wondered. They'd had some nice times together, but it wasn't any big thing. "It's not like he's my soulmate," Rachel said aloud, then stopped, mid-thought, and turned her mind in a different direction.

It's because of Frank, she typed, realizing as she did so that it was true. *It's what Frank would do. He would come to me, all apologetic for whatever he had done. He would seem so loving. Perhaps giving me flowers or gifts or one of those cards.* Rachel tensed as she wrote, unacknowledged anger filling her body. *He made me feel so loved. But just long enough for me to forgive him, for me to let him into my heart again. And then...and then he would run away again. And I would chase after him.* As she wrote, Rachel suddenly saw this pattern all too clearly. Why hadn't she ever noticed it before? Why had she let him manipulate her for so long? Why had she felt like she needed him so?

I needed him to make me feel needed, she wrote. *I always thought I wanted to feel loved, but that's not quite it. I wanted to feel needed. And Frank needed me. Whether or not he always loved me–or ever loved me, for that matter–I always knew that he needed me. He needed me to clean up his messes for him. To call into work for him and make excuses. To support us when he lost another job. To take care of him when he had a hangover. To take his beatings when he'd had too much to drink.* Again, Rachel stopped short, realizing what she'd written only after it was on the screen. "I let him beat me because I thought he needed me to," she said aloud, appalled at herself. "I let him beat me because it made me feel needed," she said again, allowing the thought to really sink home. The tears, the ones she thought she had run out of last night, came again now.

They started to fall in earnest, running down her face and landing on her keyboard. She quickly wiped them away. "I don't want to mess up my laptop," she told the empty cabin. "No tears on the typewriter." Rachel giggled at that. "Tears on the Typewriter" sounded like the title of a song. But she didn't have a typewriter, of course. She had a laptop... but when she looked down again, she found that she was looking at a typewriter. And there were tears landing on it. Annie's tears.

Annie typed slowly, deliberately.

Dear Sirs,

I regret to inform you that I must resign my position as teacher effective immediately, as I am no longer qualified to hold this position.

Annie stared at the paper, wondering if there was anything else she should say. But there wasn't really any point. She had tried to keep the pregnancy hidden as long as she could. But by now, the rumors were flying all around the town. She didn't need to explain to the school board why she had to resign from her position—they, like everyone else, already knew the truth. Annie was a "fallen woman." The fact that they hadn't fired her already was surprising. Perhaps it was only because school had already been let out for summer. It was only a matter of time. Annie felt that, at the very least, she could resign from the position, rather than let them fire her. She would do her best to keep her head held high for as long as she could, at least.

Annie shrugged. No, there was nothing else to say. She might as well close off the letter and be done with it.

Sincerely,
Annie

As she was typing, the door to her room flew open and Mr. Wallace loomed in the doorway. Without thinking, Annie turned back to her typing for a second to press "control-s" and save the work she'd done so far.

Wallace looked Annie up and down, stopping a long time to stare at her belly. Even sitting at her desk, there was a clearly defined bump. "I thought you were a good girl," he accused her. "A proper lady. I respected you. I kept away from you because I thought..." he stopped talking and stepped into her room, closing the door behind him.

Annie tried her best to remain calm. "Don't come any closer or I'll scream," she warned him. "You don't want to scare Sissy, do you?"

Wallace just laughed. "Sissy's not here. She's spending the night at the neighbor's, helping out with a sick baby. It's just the two of us, all night long..." He sneered, looking her up and down. It was clear from the way he looked what he had in mind. "All this time you were living under my roof and I could have been..." He stopped talking then, and grabbed Annie by the wrist, dragging her towards the bed in an effort to show her exactly what he could have been doing all this time.

She grabbed her fist with her other hand and, using

the leverage of both arms, pulled down, towards the floor. "His thumb is the weakest part of his grip," she told herself, not sure where she had gained that knowledge, but glad when it worked. Her wrist slipped through his thumb and she was free of his hold.

She threw the door open and ran, down the stairs, out the front door, and just kept running. In her mind she was thinking, "Call 9-1-1! Call 9-1-1!" She had no idea what this strange code meant. Instead, she called to Jebediah. Not aloud, but in her mind, she silently screamed out his name. "Jeb! Jebediah! Please come help me! Help me!"

She would have been fine, perhaps, if she hadn't tripped just as she got to the hay field. If she hadn't gone face-first to the ground, with her skirts flying up over her head. If she hadn't given him time to catch up.

He came up behind her with a sneer. "That's more like it," he said. "Positioned just right." He was on her before she could move. She screamed, but doubted that anyone could hear her. The Wallace farm was large and no one had a reason to be nearby this late at night.

The only thing she could think, over and over again, was "Protect the baby. Protect the baby!" So Annie did the last thing she wanted to do, the only thing she could do—she knelt on all fours, propping herself up by her elbows, backside high in the air to keep her belly from being pushed into the ground. And she let him do what he wanted.

"I ain't going where no baby is," Wallace announced,

as if talking to himself. "But you got other places I can go in..." Then he grabbed her firmly by the hips and jammed himself in between her buttocks.

It wasn't anything like it had been with Jeb. It wasn't a tender joining of two bodies, two souls. It was the forcing of one into another, into a spot where it clearly didn't fit.

Annie would have screamed out in pain, if her mind was still connected to her body, if she still had any control over her physical self. But she didn't. All she could do was silently scream "No! No! NO!"

With each thrust, her mind pulled further and further away. Rising from her body, away from the pain. She saw herself for a moment, as if seeing someone else. She was behind them both, observing them as if watching farm animals in the spring, as if it was happening to a body that wasn't hers anymore. She forced herself to turn around, to look the other way.

What she saw almost shocked her back into her body. It was herself—in a different face, with different eyes, but she knew it was her all the same. She was dressed as a boy, in jeans and a flannel shirt. And she had a strange-looking device on her lap, like a typewriter but flat. She was able to see that much before she was yanked back across time, back into her own body with a slap...

With the slap across her rump that Wallace gave her when he was done. "Now that's more like it," he said. "As long as you're living under my roof, you'll take care of me, you whore. You hear me?"

That slap didn't just bring her back to her body—it awoke something in her, a strength she didn't know she had. It also brought back an awareness of her surroundings, including the rock by her right hand. Without giving herself time to think, in one fluid motion, she grabbed the rock, turned around, and smashed it into Wallace's head.

He fell instantly.

Annie looked at his body, laying there in the moonlight, pants still around his ankles, blood streaming from his head. Annie knew without question: he was dead.

"I...I killed him," she said to herself in dismay. "I never meant to..." Then another thought came to her mind. "I have to get out of here. If they find me, they'll arrest me for murder."

Spurred on by the thought of getting away, she ran back into the farmhouse and quickly began to pack her carpet bag with the few possessions she owned: her other dress, her hairbrush, and the journal that Jeb had given her. She wanted to bring her typewriter along—it cost her a lot to buy and she would miss not having it. But it was also heavy, and Annie knew she wasn't going to be settling down any time soon.

Just as she was finishing up, Annie heard someone coming through the farmhouse door. She tensed, afraid it was Wallace, somehow back for more. Or perhaps the

Sheriff, come to arrest her for murder. But then she heard his voice, a voice so tender and gentle it ran through her in an instant. "Annie?" it said. "Annie, are you okay?" Jebediah had come for her. She ran down the stairs, carpet bag in hand, and threw herself into his arms.

"Mr. Wallace, he...he tried to...he..." that was all Annie could say, but it was enough.

"No," Jebediah told her firmly. "He won't do that to you. I won't let him."

Annie started to sob again, crying the tears she thought she'd already spent. "But he...already...did...and...then I...I hit him. With a rock. Hard. He's...he's dead."

She couldn't say more, but Jeb understood all too well. Wallace had hurt his Annie, hurt her in the worst way imaginable. And she had done what she needed to do. But would others see it that way?

"I have to leave," Annie said. "They'll come after me. They'll call me a murderer."

"It was self-defense," Jebediah replied. "Surely they will be able to see that."

Annie shook her head. "Who would believe me? A teacher, an unmarried woman? A pregnant unmarried woman? Mr. Wallace was a respected member of the community. On the school board. As for me...I am nothing."

"You are something to me," Jebediah replied. "You are everything to me."

He held her tight, to comfort her, to comfort himself. And as he held her, he made a plan.

"We're leaving this place together," he told her, once her shaking slowed down. "Right now. I wasn't able to protect you from this..." Jeb's voice caught as he said it, but he quickly got himself back in control, "but I will protect you from everything else. Good thing I brought this with me," he added, patting his hip. Annie noticed that he had a pistol hanging there. "I got it after our encounter with the bear. I didn't want anything to happen to hurt my Annie..." He turned away then, so Annie wouldn't see the tears in his eyes.

Without another word, he led her away from the farmhouse, away from the town, away from their old life, and into the unknown.

As the two walked into their future, I watched over them, protecting them as best I could. And wishing them a safe journey.

Rachel came out of her memory (that's how she thought about it now) shivering with fear. She had been there, she had been Annie, as Wallace had tried to force himself on her. And when he caught up to her again. And when she flew from her own body, when she turned and saw... "Me," Rachel said aloud. "She was looking at me!"

Rachel felt shaken, unhinged from the real world. How could...? Across time?

There was only one thing she could think to do—throw herself back into the real world with gusto. She would go to town. She would go shopping, the day after Christmas, in the midst of the gift-returning madness. If that didn't bring her back to the "real world," nothing would.

Granted, she lived in the U.P. It wasn't like they even had a mall or anything. But there were enough people at the outlet stores to bring her back to the present. And none of them, she concluded, seemed to be happy. Maybe all the happy people stayed home today, enjoying their gifts and their families. It was just the unhappy ones who had ventured out, to return the gifts they weren't happy with, or perhaps to get away from the families they didn't want to be around anymore. Rachel felt like, if she just spent a few minutes watching each person, she could tell their life story, just by the look on their face. But she didn't want to try. She didn't want to focus on the negative.

Finally, she came across one happy face—Sara Jacobs, the school counselor. "Hello there, Rachel," Sara said as soon as she saw her. "I see you decided to brave the day, too."

Rachel smiled at her. She didn't want to say that she had left the house to get away from the memories—her own and Annie's—that were haunting her.

"I had to run to the store to get more oil for my latkes,"

Sara explained, "for our Hanukkah dinner tonight. I can't believe I didn't check that ahead of time!"

"Oh, um, happy Hanukkah," Rachel replied. "I didn't realize you were Jewish."

Sara smiled. "Yeah, there's not a lot of us up here in the U.P. but we few are strong. Hey, if you don't have any other plans, would you like to join us for dinner? The more the merrier! Seriously!"

Rachel's first reaction was to say no, to make up some reason why she was too busy. But the truth was, she wasn't busy. And it would be good for her to be around someone else for a while.

"I guess it would be alright. Maybe one of my new Christmas traditions could be to eat Hanukkah dinner with you," Rachel replied and smiled. It seemed like another perfect way to celebrate the season.

She had a wonderful evening with Sara and her extended family—her husband, her grown children, and her grandchildren. They shared stories, they shared laughter, they shared the latkes and the brisket and the challah, the traditional baked bread. They even had an extra menorah for Rachel to light. She felt happy. She felt like she belonged. And she felt sad, at the same time. This was the kind of family Rachel had always dreamed of being a part of. She enjoyed the night, but it was bittersweet, too. It reminded her of what she'd never had before.

When she finally left and was walking to her car to

drive home, she felt more alone than she'd ever felt before. "It's a good thing I have you with me," Rachel said to the moon that was peeking through the clouds at her. "It seems like you are always there when I need you."

I try to be, I answered back. Whenever you need me most, I will always try to be there for you.

Chapter 6

Annie and Jebediah walked for a long time in silence. Annie had no idea where they were going or what her life would be like from now on, but Jebediah seemed to have a plan. Annie was content to follow him, content to not have to figure this all out on her own.

They walked through the night and into the next morning. Annie was tired and sore and hungry and her stomach was acting up again. Finally, she had to stop and go behind a tree so she could throw up, her new morning ritual. She felt embarrassed doing it with Jebediah around, but she didn't really have a choice.

"I'm sorry I did this to you," Jebediah told her when she returned to him. "I should have been a more honorable man and left you alone, but..."

Annie took his hand in hers. "You didn't do this to me. We did it together. It was what we both wanted. And we will get through this together, somehow."

"Together forever," Jebediah agreed. "Come on," he

added, taking her hand and starting to walk again. "We're almost there now."

Annie could hear the sound of running water—lots of running water. The closer they got, the louder it grew, until it was almost a roar. Then the trees opened up a bit and Annie could see why. They had come to a giant waterfall. It looked like a great wall of water, longer than any building Annie had seen, even before she'd come to the rugged wilderness of the Upper Peninsula.

Then she saw a half dozen log cabins dotted near the shore of the river, just below the falls. Annie looked at Jebediah, questioningly.

Jebediah smiled at her confusion, happy to be able to share his secret with her. "The Indians used this village when they wanted to be close to the falls, but that was before the white man's treaties took the land away from them and forced them to move. I know it's a strange place to take you, but I wasn't sure where else to go and I knew these cabins were here and we could stay here until we think of what to do next."

Annie smiled and hugged Jebediah. "It's perfect," she reassured him.

Jebediah smiled, happy that Annie was happy. But he knew these cabins were less than perfect. He explained to Annie that they had been standing abandoned for years, since the Indians had been forced to forgo their traditional way of life and live just outside the white men's villages. There they worked in the lumber mills, mines, and fisheries, all year round, in a vain effort to supply their families with enough food to eat. Once, these forests had been teaming with wildlife for them to hunt; once the rivers and lakes had been filled with fish for them to catch. Only thirty or forty years before, the Indians had been able to live off the land as their ancestors had for thousands of years. Now, they were treated as third-class citizens, barely scraping by with low paying jobs, while they watched these "newcomers" take over the land that had once been theirs. And yet, they always tried to treat the white man with kindness, no matter how they were treated in return.

Once, Jebediah had asked one of the natives about it. "After all we have done to you, to your land and the animals and fish, why do you still treat us with such kindness?"

He had smiled, gently. "We Anishinabe—the first people—we knew you were coming," he explained. "There was a prophecy of the visitors who would come to this land. There were signs. The men who first came wore the cross, like our own medicine wheel. The white man and the Anishinabe, we are all one family, the human family. The prophecy tells us this."

If true, then Jebediah was thankful for his brothers leaving these cabins here, a place where he could take Annie while they struggled to plan their future. He wished that he had his own prophecy, to tell him what that was.

For now, he was just glad to have someplace to take her, somewhere she could lay down and sleep for a while. Even with cracks in the walls where the mud had dried and fallen out, even with dirt covering the floor and the ceiling partially caved in, it provided a roof over her head and walls to surround her. It was enough for now.

Rachel hadn't heard from James all week, ever since Christmas day. To be honest, part of her was glad of it and tempted to just leave well enough alone. She was embarrassed about what had happened. Not the fact that they had sex—she was a grown woman, after all, and she could choose to have sex with another consenting adult if she wanted to without feeling guilty about it...or at least too guilty about it. But what really bothered her was why she had done it, and the distance that had been between them. If there really was a distinction between "having sex" and "making love," well, they had not made love. It was more of a mutual use thing. And that's what bothered Rachel. It was better, after all, not to have to face him ever again.

And yet...there had been something growing between the two of them, something much more special than "mutual use." And Rachel couldn't bring herself to give up on that something.

So she sent him a text, asking him if he wanted to do a

ballroom dancing class with her. It was a long shot. What guy was going to agree to take a dance class? But it was something she'd always wanted to do and she'd seen this flyer at work about it and...and what the heck? It didn't hurt—too much—to ask.

He replied with a yes.

And that's how she found herself, the next Tuesday night, with James and about five other couples, at a dance studio, waiting nervously to find out what they had gotten themselves into.

The instructor introduced himself, talked a little bit about the history of ballroom dancing, explained that they were going to focus on doing swing style, then demonstrated the basic hold position.

If Rachel had felt tension before, just being close to James, it was nothing like she felt now, having him hold her in a room full of other people. They got into the position and held it there until the instructor came around and confirmed that they were doing it right. As soon as he moved on, they let go of each other and took a step apart to take away some of the intensity.

But before long, Rachel was so busy learning the dance moves, and helping James learn his moves, that she forgot her embarrassment. The tension between them had melted away. She relaxed and started to enjoy the feeling of being in James' arms. Nothing awkward, nothing even sexual. Just comforting.

"Do you want to go get a beer?" James asked Rachel after the class was over. They went to a local bar and had a beer and talked for a long time. When he finally dropped her back at the cabin, James gave her a goodnight kiss. Nothing else, for now. Rachel had a feeling that they would sleep together again, but not until they were ready. And when they were both really ready, she knew things would be different.

It had been a while since Rachel had gone to the second-hand store—since before Christmas. She didn't really need anything else. But she felt called to go, anyway. She never knew what she might find. And to be honest, as the winter months started to drag on, Rachel was looking for something—anything—to get excited over. Maybe an unexpected find would do that. She had no idea just how right she was.

"I have something that might interest you," the store owner said as soon as Rachel walked in. "It came in right after Christmas, and I've been holding onto it for you ever since. I didn't put it on the shelf because I didn't want anyone else to buy it. I just knew you had to see this." He reached under the counter and pulled out a small, leather-bound book, which he handed to Rachel.

As she took it, a strange feeling came over her, as if she

already knew the book somehow. She half expected to be transported, once again, to Annie's time, and she mentally braced herself for the "trip." But nothing happened.

Carefully, she looked all around the cover. The leather was old and faded but there was no sign of any kind of markings on it. The pages along the edge were yellowed with age. She gently opened the book. Inside, the pages were covered with handwriting—small, delicate words, written close together with no margins, as if the person writing it were trying to save space.

Rachel turned to the first page and began to read.

March 18, 1896
Dear Diary,

My name is Annie and I live in the upper peninsula of the state of Michigan in the United States of America, along the giant lake that the Indians around here refer to as Gitchigumi, the Great Lake. I moved up here last fall to be a teacher. And now, I am in love. I can't tell anyone. If they knew, I would lose my teaching job. But here, in this diary that only I will see, I can admit the truth—I am in love with Jebediah Jones.

Rachel smiled, remembering when she had gotten the book, what had happened that day, and why she had written what she did in here. She remembered how much she had been overflowing with love for Jebediah that day and how she wanted to shout it from the rooftops but could only write it down here, in her diary. She smiled to herself at the memory of it all. Then blushed, suddenly remembering that she was Rachel, not Annie, living in the twenty-first century, not back in 1896. And the store-owner must be wondering what was going on in her head.

"Um, yeah, very interesting," she said, trying to cover up her embarrassment. "How much would you like for it?" She reached into her purse to pull out her wallet.

The store-owner smiled. "It's so hard to put a price on something personalized like that. I probably should donate it to a museum or something, but..." he looked at Rachel and winked. "How about I just give it to you?"

"Really?" Rachel asked, unable to mask her delight. "I mean, are you sure? I could..."

The store owner just nodded. "I knew it was meant for you the moment I got it. It belongs to you. I can't charge you for something that already belongs to you."

Rachel thanked the store-owner again, wondering if he had any idea how right he was. Then she raced back to her cabin, eager to read her—Annie's—diary and see what other secrets it contained.

Rachel read long into the night, flipping quickly over the parts of the story she already knew. She wanted to find out what happened to Annie and Jebediah after they'd left town.

June 19, 1896

We only stayed in the Indian cabin a few days. I'd like to say that it was a wonderfully romantic time, just me and Jebediah alone together at last. Perhaps it would have been, if it weren't for the black flies and the mosquitos. Between them, we never were really alone together. They were everywhere, day and night, buzzing in our ears, biting us, making us itch. The cabin walls, with the cracks where the mud had dried and fallen out, were no barrier for them.

Plus, we were hungry. Jebediah tried to hunt, but he could barely find anything. He was finally able to catch a squirrel, which he skinned and roasted over the fire. But I couldn't eat it. I wanted to, but my stomach wouldn't let me. I threw up after I took my first bite. The baby didn't want squirrel meat–it wanted bread.

That's when we knew it was time to move on. We headed back toward civilization. Kind of. We went to live with the Indians.

Perhaps it was an odd choice. We could have walked a little further, gone to live with "our people" in the next town. If we claimed we were already married, nobody would think twice about the baby. We could find a minister who would marry us in secret and all would be fine.

But we didn't do that. I was still shaken up by what had

happened with Mr. Wallace. Honestly, I didn't want to see an-other white man—other than Jeb—for a long, long time. And as for Jebediah, he had his own reasons for wanting to avoid the white man. I think he just knew too much. When he worked at the lumber mill, while the other men avoided the Indian workers, he talked to them. He learned their stories. He heard what the white man had done—and was still doing—to their way of life. And he took it to heart. We talked about it, on the long walk from the cabin by the waterfall, and we both agreed. The Indians might not have much, but what they did have—knowledge of the land and respect for all that was living on it—was more important to us than anything else.

I could tell, as he told me of the Indians, how bad he felt about what was happening to them. I felt it, too. I had always admired those who were brave enough to leave the comfort of the cities down south and come to this remote location to try to build a life. It was why I took the job teaching here. But now, I had to wonder what the cost was. I had thought of this peninsula as a vast wilderness. I had not realized that it was already someone's home.

Rachel quickly flipped to the next journal entry, to find out more.

June 24, 1896
When we got to the village, we went to the home of Bill "the Bear" LaPaire. His wife, Minnie, was known as a midewiwin, or medicine woman. She spoke to me, asking many questions.

She felt my stomach, where the baby was growing. Then she nodded. "It is good," she said in English to me–all the Indians in the village knew and spoke English, and many of them could even read and write it. "You are young and healthy and strong. You will survive this pregnancy." Instead of feeling better, I felt instantly scared. I knew, of course, that many women died in childbirth. But I hadn't thought of that–hadn't let myself think of that–until now. I think Jebediah had the same realization, because I saw him turn pale. Then he went outside with Bear for a long time. When he came back in, he told me we would be staying here, close to Minnie, until after the baby was born. And through the winter, to make sure both me and the baby stayed healthy.

I looked around the small one-room shack, covered with tar paper on the outside and lined with newspapers on the inside, and wondered where exactly we would stay. They brought in a bed for us to use for now, but Jebediah had a plan, to help us all long term.

He got a job at the lumber mill south of the village. He saved most of the money he made, but he also spent a little of it right where he worked, buying some of the lumber he cut and other building supplies. He was always on the look-out for scrap lumber, things that they couldn't ship and sell. They let him have that for free. He explained to me once that, if he had dark skin and black hair, they would have said he was lazy and looking for handouts, but since he was white, they called him industrious. They didn't realize it was going to help the Indian village, anyway.

Before long, Jeb had built an addition to Bear and Minnie's small home, where we could live. He wanted me close to Minnie at all times until the baby was born and we knew for sure I would survive. That was fine with me. I enjoyed the presence of the older woman and I learned so much from her. How to cook rice and beans and squash over an open fire. How to make bannock— their traditional bread, which is what was finally able to settle my stomach and prevent the morning sickness. She taught me how to make moccasins and even how to add complex beadwork. But more than that, she taught me about life.

And on another page:

September 10, 1896
I used to dream about getting married someday, like my older sister did. Her wedding was a big occasion. Everyone in town came, bringing their best china to eat on. There were cakes and chickens and lemonade and all kinds of good things to eat. There were flowers everywhere. And she even had a dress made just for the occasion—a fancy blue dress with a bustle and lace edging. They had a fiddler playing and everyone danced. And I thought, "This is exactly what I want on my wedding day."
Instead, today Jebediah and I went together to the local county seat for the first time. It wasn't the same county where I'd taught, but I kept expecting to see a wanted poster with my face on it for the murder of Mr. Wallace. We went to the courthouse and asked to get a marriage license. I pretended that I didn't

notice the man looking at my belly. Instead, I just held my head high. It probably wasn't the first time he'd seen a pregnant bride, and I doubted it would be his last. Either way, he got us the piece of paper and we signed it and that was that. Not the kind of wedding I had once dreamed about, but it didn't really matter. I was now Jebediah's wife, and that was what counted.

Rachel read on to the next entry...

November 29, 1896

It is winter now. Jeb worked hard all fall at the lumber mill and around the village. After he finished the addition to Bear and Minnie's place, he moved on to other homes in the village, fixing them and adding to them where he could. At first, the other Indians in the village didn't want to let him help. They didn't want to "take a white man's handouts." But Bear spoke to each of them, one at a time. He explained that Jeb was not a "white man." He has, as Bear put it, "the heart of an Anishinabe." And so do I.

Now that it's winter, it's the season for storytelling. Bear and Minnie take turns telling us the stories of their ancestors, the humorous tales of Nanabozho, the trickster god who created the animals as we know them today and whose stories contain many lessons on life. Both Bear and Minnie seem very intent on making sure we learn these stories, so we can tell them to our children—Minnie is certain that this baby is only the first of many—as they grow. But we have also been warned to only tell the stories during the winter. *This is the time for the telling of stories. And everything must be done in its proper time and place.*

It took four rings of Rachel's cell phone before she was able to register what the sound was—she was so lost in Annie's world. But once she finally realized what it was, she scrambled to answer it.

"Hi, Rachel," the voice on the other end said. "It's Tim. I just thought I'd call and see how things are going."

"Tim," Rachel replied happily. "The craziest thing has happened to me. Do you have time for me to tell you about it?"

"I have all the time in the world for you," Tim replied on the other end.

"Well," Rachel began, "I was at this second-hand store the other day, and the owner gave me this old book. A journal written by a woman who lived back in the late 1800's." Rachel told her brother all about the adventures of Annie and Jebediah. She didn't mention the memories she'd been having about their lives—that was too weird to share with anyone—but she did tell him what she'd learned from the diary. It was nice to share it with someone else in her own time period. She didn't feel quite so crazy that way.

Chapter 7

Rachel woke up in the middle of the night with almost unbearable pains in her stomach. Well, actually a bit lower. There was only one thing it could be—contractions. If Rachel didn't know any better, she would have rushed herself off to the hospital to deliver a baby. Except she wasn't the one having the baby—Annie was.

"Just how connected am I to her?" Rachel wondered aloud. Then another contraction came along and she couldn't think about anything else.

In between contractions, she lay in her bed, trying to do breathing exercises to help her relax. She closed her eyes, focusing her thoughts on breathing slowly in and out, in and out. When she opened her eyes again, she was seeing the world through Annie's eyes.

She was in the room that Jebediah had built for them. Minnie was with her but the men had been told to stay away. Rachel—Annie—wanted to lie down, to relax between contractions, but Minnie wouldn't let her. "If you lay down, the baby will never come out," she said over and over. "Keep walking, keep moving, to help the baby out."

She also gave Annie a mixture of chokeberries and other herbs to help with the delivery, although Annie wasn't sure if it was to help speed up the delivery, take away some of the pain, or just part of the birth ritual. She was finding it hard to think about anything at all, except the pain.

"I can't do this," she said aloud, over and over again. "I can't, I can't do this."

"Of course you can," Minnie replied in a calm, soothing voice. "You are a woman, like our Mother Earth. You were made to create new life. You were born for this."

"I can't, I... oh, it's coming," she said suddenly.

"Come over here," Minnie told her, still very calm. She led Annie to an area in the room where leaves had been spread out on the dirt floor and told her to squat down. Annie did, finding the position quite natural.

The head seemed to take forever to pass, but once it was through, the rest of the body just slipped out. It fell, not into Minnie's hands, as Annie had expected, but onto the pile of leaves, caught by Mother Earth herself. Only then did Minnie step in, cutting the umbilical cord, rubbing the baby down with ashes, and wrapping it tightly in a blanket.

"Your own little girl," Minnie said as she handed

the baby to the new mother. "Teach her well the ways of our people. Then, like you and Jebediah, she will be Anishinabe, one of the first people. And then she can pass that knowledge on to the next seven generations to come."

Rachel came out of the "memory" with a jolt. "Seven generations to come." That was what Minnie had said to Annie. Rachel had heard this idea before. When the Anishinabe made big decisions, like when they were making treaties with the American government, they always tried to consider what affect it would have on their children seven generations later.

Rachel tried to do the math in her head. "Annie had her baby in 1896. So Annie is the first generation and her baby girl is the second generation. And maybe she had a kid of her own about twenty years later, that would put it at... 1906... wait, no 1916. Right during World War I. And then another twenty years or so to 1936. That would be the 4th generation. Then the fifth would be about 1956. My mom was born in 1960. That would make me the sixth generation. Is that right? Wait, she was born in...oh, I don't know. Something like that. I guess the seventh generation will never come," Rachel added, thinking of the little baby she never had, never could have now.

And the tears started to fall once again. For the baby

she lost years ago and for the chance for any future babies. There would be no seventh generation because her line would end with her. All because of Frank and his temper...

The knock on the door startled Rachel so much she almost jumped out of her skin. She half expected to see Frank at the door, so strong had his memory been in her mind. Every muscle in her body tensed up.

"It can't be him," she told herself, trying to talk her own emotions down. "It won't be him. Why would it be? I am free now. I am safe here." She took a deep breath, wiped away her tears, and went to the door.

What—who—she found instead was James.

"I...ah...I know it's the middle of the night and I... hopefully I didn't wake you, but...I... Honestly, I don't know why I am here. I just felt like...I felt like you needed me and..." As his voice trailed off, Rachel ushered him inside.

He was clearly embarrassed about being there in the middle of the night. And yet, he was right. Rachel had needed him, needed someone to talk to, someone who would listen to everything—the whole story of Annie and her flashbacks as well as the truth about Frank and his temper—and not think she was totally crazy. In the light of day, she would never have dared to tell anyone all of this.

But in the middle of the night, after the almost physical exhaustion of remembering Annie giving birth, after the emotional exhaustion of remembering Frank, and the fall, and the reason she would never give birth herself, all of her walls were down. James was a listening ear and Rachel had a million stories that needed telling.

They sat on the couch while she talked, first on opposite ends, but before long, Rachel was snuggled against James, cuddling in his arms. And later, when Rachel had told James everything she could think of, when her mind was finally at peace again, they both stood up, without saying a word, and pulled out the hide-a-bed. Rachel went into her room to grab the pillow from off her bed, along with the bedspread.

When she came back, she found James stoking the fire. She smiled at him and he smiled in return. Then he took her hand and led her to the couch-bed. They climbed in together and Rachel covered them both with her comforter. Then James put his arm around her, pulled her close, and covered her with his comfort. And like that, they fell asleep.

Again, I shined through the window, watching them, closer together than they had ever been—even when they'd had sex. It was a gamble, waking James up in the middle of the night and giving him the urge to drive over to her cabin. Would he actually do it? How would she respond to seeing him at her door? And yet, I knew the timing was right. Her defenses were down. And I knew her honesty would break through the last of his defenses. Besides, they had been apart for far too long this lifetime. They needed each other, and it was up to me to make sure they saw that.

Some people say that the full moon causes madness, but it's not madness at all. What I do is help people to realize what they have tried so hard to hide from themselves. I bring out their sanity in a world that wants to keep them insane. What others call madness is actually someone just finally living their truth.

It felt so natural for Rachel to wake up in James' arms. Not like sleeping with Frank had been. For years, Rachel had made sure to fall asleep before Frank came to bed, so she wouldn't have to deal with the uncomfortableness of having him so near. But with James, she wanted to stay awake and next to him forever. She felt so...safe.

As she lay there savoring the feeling, she thought about the events of the night before, about how she had been able to open up to James. She had never opened up that much to anyone before. And he had believed her, even when she told him about Annie and her memories. It felt so wonderful to be believed.

Frank had been doubtful and suspicious of everything she did or said. How many times had she hurried to get her work done at school, because she knew if she stayed too late, Frank would accuse her of having an affair. As if she'd even had time for such a thing! When she did come home late, he would actually smell her, to see if he could detect any "man smell" on her. She was just starting to realize how much of what she did in life was based on a fear of what Frank might suspect that she was doing, instead. And now, she was with a man who believed her, not just about normal things like what she had done during the day. He had believed her when she told him that she could remember a past life. It was such a comforting feeling!

There was another feeling she had, as she lay on the hide-a-bed next to his warm body. When she felt him start to wake up, she pressed her own body against his, to see if he had a similar feeling. He responded in kind. And this time, their love-making (which it truly was this time) brought them even closer.

It was a long winter for Annie, even with the excitement of a new baby. Or perhaps because of the new baby. Her daughter was growing well, was thriving in every way. She was the apple of Jebediah's eye and had charmed her way into Minnie's and even Bear's affections. Annie was delighted by her daughter, too. And yet...

All Annie really wanted to do was lay on the sleeping

platform in their room. She wanted to sleep and perhaps never wake up. She was worried. Jebediah was worried. But Minnie was not worried. She had overseen enough births in her life, comforted enough new mothers, to know what was happening to Annie. She might not have known the terms "postpartum depression," but she knew all about the sadness that sometimes came with childbirth. Rather than focusing on helping Annie, Minnie began to pray about her baby, to ask the ancestors to help guide her to a name for the child. The naming ceremony would help the baby to become part of the tribe, would help her all her life to know who she was and what she had been called to do. But the ceremony would also help Annie, Minnie knew, to leave the shadow world of sadness behind and to come back into the world of the living.

It didn't take long for Minnie to get the vision. The baby was Mashkikiik-Giizis, Healing Moon. It was she that would heal her mother's sadness, Minnie saw, as she would heal many others throughout her life. But she would not be a medicine woman, as Minnie was, who heals the sickness of the body. Instead, she would work to heal the sicknesses of the heart.

They had the naming ceremony not long after Minnie's vision. Several members of the tribe, both male and female, were chosen to be the child's we-eh, which are like god-parents. They agreed to watch over, protect, and advise the child throughout her life. In addition, Minnie would be her Nookomis, her grandmother, and Bear would be her grandfather, her Nimishomis. If anything ever happened to Annie and Jebediah, their child would always have a home in the tribe and a family to care for her. She would never be alone.

The ceremony itself was held in the Great Lodge, the only place large enough for the whole tribe to gather in the cold of winter. And everyone in the tribe wanted to be there to welcome the new child into their community. Annie was worried that some of the tribe would not want to allow a white child to become one of them. But her fears were unfounded. It was Bear who explained it to her. They did not see this baby as a white child or an Indian child—they saw her as a bridge, bringing the two worlds together as one. Bear knew that she would likely live in the white man's world when she grew up. But she would not—could not now—forget the part of her that belonged to the Anishinabe. She was of the first people just as surely as if she had been Bear's biological granddaughter.

And so they gathered. They watched as Annie and Jebediah gave gifts of tobacco to Minnie for her role in naming their child. And then they gave their as-yet-unnamed baby to the medicine woman. Minnie spoke for a while, both in Anishinabe and in English, explaining her vision. Finally, she told the people, told Annie and Jebediah, and told their daughter her name. "She is Mashkikiik-Giizis, Healing Moon," Minnie told everyone.

"She will heal the souls and hearts of many throughout her life. She will help to bring people back to the peace of understanding of who we are and our place in the universe." She kissed the child gently on her cheek, then passed her to her first we-eh who repeated the process and passed her on. It was only after each we-eh had a chance to say her name, approve of it, and kiss her on her little cheek, that Annie was finally allowed to hold her daughter, her Healing Moon.

"Yes," Annie said to the people. "This is Mashkikiik-Giizis, the Healing Moon. And she has already begun to heal me."

And I looked upon the gathering, smiling down on my namesake. Yes, Mashkikiik-Giizis would heal many. Just as I have always done.

And then, after everyone had a chance to hold little Kiki, as she was soon called, the party really began. At first, Annie was surprised by all the excitement around Kiki's naming. But then she realized that, in the middle of January, the tribe was happy to have anyone—anything—to celebrate. It gave them a chance to get out of their own huts for a while, to get together, to eat well, and to dance.

The drum had been set up in the center of the room

and men surrounded it, drumming in time and singing. Behind them, women also sang. And around the group in the middle, always in a clockwise direction, the people danced. They danced in joy of a new member coming to their tribe, danced in celebration of their old ways, and danced to hide from the realities of their lives in the present.

Annie loved these people and admired the way they had been able to hold on to the customs of the past. But she was not blind, either. Their homes were small and falling apart, despite what Jebediah did to try to fix them. Money was tight and they learned to live without. Many men had to leave the community and travel to work in sawmills and in fishing, or travel deep into the forest, where they could find jobs in logging. Sometimes, they were able to make a little money with trapping. The things that they had once done with ease, in harmony with the world around them, they now struggled to do for others, with hopes of only a small payment in return for their work. They were being forced to help over-fish and over-hunt and over-cut the land their ancestors had spent centuries protecting.

And then, as Minnie had explained to Annie, there was the whiskey. Bear and many of the other elders fought hard to keep whiskey away from their community. But it was a losing battle. The white men would offer whiskey as a form of payment for the furs or fish the Anishinabe caught. Or the white workers would share some with the Indians good-naturedly. It didn't really matter how Minnie's people first got a taste of whiskey—the effects were the same. The white men were used to alcohol—their ancestors had been partaking of it for generations upon generations. But for the Anishinabe, who had never known it before, the effect was multiplied. There was no one at the naming celebration that was intoxicated (they knew enough to keep that away from something so sacred) but Annie had heard stories about "the drunken Indian," back when she was still teaching school. The townspeople liked to joke about how "them Indians can't hold their liquor." Now Annie understood why.

Annie thought about all this as she watched her new tribe dance to the beat of the dewe'igan, the drum. Then a young girl came up to her, smiling, and pulled her into the dance. Annie tried to copy the movements of the other women's feet. The girl smiled at Annie, encouraging her, and then showed her exactly what to do.

"Feel the drum," the young girl instructed Annie. "Step to the beat of the drum. That is the heartbeat of our people. Dance to the heartbeat."

Annie closed her eyes, concentrating on feeling the drumbeat, allowing her body to move up and down in time to the beat. Then she moved her feet, as well, taking a step with each beat. The more she did, the more natural it felt.

Just then, someone rushed into the community room, screaming, "Run, children. It's the Saggardiboanyawek!"

The girl that Annie was dancing with grabbed her hand and started to run towards the back exit. Annie glanced quickly over to where Minnie was holding Kiki's cradle board, then followed the girl outside and into the night.

They ran for a long time before the girl finally felt safe enough to stop.

"What was that?" Annie asked her companion.

"The Saggardiboanyawek were coming for us. We had to hide before they could grab us."

"The what?" Annie asked, confused.

The girl smiled at her confusion, but then grew instantly serious as she explained. "Saggardiboanyawek. It means 'the ones who pull you by the hair.' They call themselves the Indian agents, but they are no agents of ours. They come to try to steal away the children."

"Steal the children..." Annie said, remembering what Jebediah had told her.

The girl nodded. "They want to take us away, send us to their boarding schools, turn us white like them. When they first came, when they said they wanted to teach us, to help us, we believed them. Some of the kids went with them. But they didn't come back. Or if they did, they were different. They would try to tell us we were wrong, that we needed to change, to be more like the white man." The girl trailed off, lost in her own thoughts for a moment. "Now, when they come, we run. We hide. We don't want to go with them. We don't want to lose who we are."

It's strange, Annie thought to herself. She was honored that little Kiki would be learning the Anishinabe culture, to become "more Indian." And yet these men were trying to make the Indian children "less Indian." Why would anyone want to make children less of what they are?

Then another thought occurred to Annie. "Why would they come for you now, in the evening, during our celebration? Why don't they just take the children while you are at school?"

The girl laughed at Annie's naiveté. "We don't have school," she explained. "Not anymore. We used to have one, but the building was old and falling apart and didn't have heat. Only the kids who had warm enough coats could even attend in the winter. And when the last teacher left, no one came to replace her. Nobody wanted to teach us—not in that old, falling down building. We kept hoping the government would build us a new school, a warm school. Instead, they built the boarding school downstate. And started taking the kids there. And... I would like to learn to read and write. But I don't want to leave my family. And I don't want to lose who I am. So when they come for me, I run and I hide, and I don't get schooling anymore."

As the girl spoke, Annie listened carefully, nodding and encouraging her. But in her mind, she was already starting to develop a plan.

Chapter 8

Towards the last few pages of the journal, Rachel saw that the entries became sporadic, as if Annie was trying to sum up months that had gone by when she was too busy to write.

October 12, 1897
Once the weather warmed up and Jebediah felt confident that both Kiki and I were going to be okay, he started building a home for us. All winter, while he had been working at the sawmill, he'd been saving most of his earnings. I added in what I had left from my year as a teacher and we used it to buy some land, just past the reservation, within sight of Gitchigumi.

Every day when Jeb got home from the sawmill, as tired as he must have been, we worked to build our home. It was small, with only two rooms. One was the living and cooking area, and the other was the bedroom. But it was ours, on our own land, and I loved it.

Rachel stopped reading for a moment, thinking about her own current home—a small cabin with only two rooms, just across the road from Lake Superior.

We finished it just as the leaves were starting to change.

The final step was to plant some flowers. I don't even know how Jeb discovered my love of daffodils, or if it was just chance, but one night he came home from the sawmill with a handful of bulbs. One of the men he worked with had given them to him—a gift from his wife to Jeb's wife. Jeb and I planted them that very day, on either side of the door.

Rachel stopped reading a moment, and looked through the front window at the patches of wild daffodils around the "lawn." Perhaps they once grew only by the door, but now they were spread out over most of the front yard. Could these be...? Rachel shook her head and turned back to reading the diary.

Then, once we had a home, I could turn my plan into a reality. Ever since the night of Kiki's naming, ever since I learned of the Saggardiboanyawek and the boarding schools, I knew that I had to help the kids of my new tribe. I was a teacher and these kids needed a school, a place where they could learn to read and write and understand the white man's ways, but where they could still learn to value their own ways, too. I didn't want to turn them into white men—I wanted to teach them how to protect themselves.

They had to be able to read the treaties that were being offered to them. They had to know how to write their own replies. And they needed to know arithmetic, to determine the value of their land, to calculate the taxes they had to pay. To protect themselves from the white men, they had to first understand their ways.

And so I quietly let it be known that any child who stopped by our home between nine and three would get lessons in these important skills. These children, in turn, were expected to teach their parents what they'd learned.

On the next page was another entry.

November 8, 1897

A strange thing happened today. While I was working with the children, there was a knock on the front door. I didn't even have to tell them to go out the back and hide in the shed. We had practiced this many times, in case the Indian Agents came for them. My heart was racing as I picked up Kiki where she had been sitting in her cradleboard, watching the lessons. Then, slowly and calmly, I walked to the front door, giving the children plenty of time to hide. What I saw when I opened the door, though, was not an Indian Agent, but another officer of the law. It was the Sheriff from the next county over, the one Jebediah and I had left in such a hurry on that fateful night.

I knew he wasn't after the children, and I was glad for that. But at the same time, I was worried for them. I feared they were about to lose their teacher. After all, if the Sheriff was here, that could only mean one thing—he was here to arrest me for the murder of Mr. Wallace. I wondered what would happen to Kiki. Would he at least let me wait until Jebediah came home before he took me away?

"Miss Annie," he said, tipping his hat. "Or should I say Mrs. now? I hear congratulations are in order." I didn't understand. His words didn't make sense to me. If he was here to arrest me, why was he congratulating me on my marriage?

"I've been looking all over for you," he continued. "Luckily the County Clerk here had heard of your situation and sent word to me when she saw your name on that marriage license. Took me a while to make it over this way. Wasn't sure how I'd find you, but the Register of Deeds remembered recording you and your husband's property purchase and was kind enough to give me the address. Anyway, I...we...we want to let you know that it's okay, that you can come back if you want, you can even be a teacher again, if you'd like to. The school board took a vote and..."

"You mean, you're not here to arrest me for killing Mr. Wallace?" I blurted out, interrupting him in his speech.

He vigorously shook his head and then a smile came over his face. A sad smile. "I know what happened, Annie. I was actually nearby that night, on my patrol, when I heard your screams off in the distance. I rushed to where the sound came from, but by the time I got there..." He paused for a moment, unsure what to say, how to bring up the delicate subject. "I found Wallace, pants around his ankles, blood running from his head. I could see the signs of a struggle. I knew at once what had happened. Oh, Miss

Annie, we are all so sorry we put you in that situation. We never suspected that he would... We're very sorry."

I stared at him, still struggling to comprehend what he was saying. "You're not going to arrest me?" I asked again, as if I just couldn't believe what I'd heard.

The Sheriff shook his head. "No, we're not. It was self-defense. Clearly. In fact, as I said, we want you back. We want you to be our teacher again."

I probably should have talked to Jeb before I answered him. After all, we could have used the extra income. But no, I did not want to move out of this wonderful little home that we'd spent so much time and effort to build. Besides, I had a new teaching job, now, with students who really needed me.

"Thank you," I told the sheriff. "I am glad to know that I won't be arrested, and I do appreciate the offer. But we are happy here, for now."

"Very well," the sheriff replied. "But if you ever need anything, please let me know. I mean it, Annie," he added, and then turned around and walked away.

As I watched him go, I felt a weight lift from my shoulders, a weight I didn't even know was there until it left. I let out a sigh, then Kiki and I went out to the shed to get the children and bring them back in for the rest of their lesson.

Rachel had now gotten to the end of the journal and read the last entry.

December 12, 1897

    I had a strange dream last night. Not a dream, really, so much as a vision. I was lying in bed, just about to fall asleep, when I heard the sound of the Indian's drums, like the drums I heard back when Jebediah and I had only just met. I tried to picture them, as I remembered them, gathered around a campfire, dancing the memorizing dance around the circle.

    I saw the familiar movements, but I saw other things, too. Girls with shiny shawls, with long fringes around them, dancing a wild step that looked like a bird or a butterfly floating through the air. Some of the girls had on dresses that were covered in silver metal bells, that clinked together as they moved up and down, creating a tinkling sound, almost like rain. A few of the boys wore traditional outfits, complete with embroidered vests and belts, a few even wearing the leggings. But there were others—girls and boys, wearing denim pants. And undershirts with brightly printed designs on them. And the shoes on their feet looked like neither moccasins nor the white-man's leather shoes, but a mix somewhere in between.

    We were not outside, either, I realized. We were in a large room, a meeting hall of some kind. But the walls were made of metal and the beams in the ceiling were metal, too. And while some of the kids were dancing, many others sat in long seats along the walls—more kids than I had seen together in my life.

    But the thing that stood out most of all, in this vision, was not what the kids were wearing or even what they were doing. It was how the children looked. There were some that were clearly

Indian—with long black hair, dark skin, and the beautiful moon-shaped faces. There were others that were just as clearly white—some with blond hair, some even with red. Then there were also many that seemed to be a mix of the two. There were even some Negro children there, as well. All dancing together, all smiling, all seeming unaware of what a strange thing this was for me, to see children from different races all dancing together as one.

Then a tall man with long hair picked up a short black stick and seemed to speak into it. As he did so, his voice echoed through the entire room. "Today, we are here to celebrate the grandfather teachings of wisdom. As our ancestors taught us, it is important to think, not just about our own lives, but also about those around us and those yet to come. When our ancestors had to make important decisions, they didn't just think about how it would affect themselves—they always considered how it would affect the next seven generations. It is because of our ancestors and their wisdom that we have this school now, where all children can come and learn about the traditions of the Anishinabe people. It is because of them that we can all be here now to dance."

I remember that I started to move out onto the floor to join the dance. A young girl with brown skin, brown eyes, and curly brown hair came up to me, smiled, and took my hand. "Perhaps she is one of my own descendants," I thought, realizing that I was seeing into the future. "Perhaps she is my great-granddaughter seven generations later. And perhaps she is no relation to me at all." But her genealogy didn't really matter. I knew, without a doubt, that she was the child of the children of the students I once *taught. And now, children of all races were dancing together. And I knew that somehow, I had had a part in making that happen.*

It was rather amazing, Rachel thought, how good James and her got along, now that they had finally both been able to let down their guard, give up their walls. It wasn't perfect, of course. There were still days when Frank haunted Rachel's mind, when she started to doubt herself, when she just knew James couldn't possibly love her, not with all her faults. Sometimes, she shared these fears with James. Sometimes, she just kept them to herself, letting them eat away at her. Until she saw James again, of course. Because the way he looked at her left no place in her mind for doubt. Each day, they learned more about each other. Each day, he witnessed more of her "faults." And he just kept loving her all the same. It was almost as if they were meant to be together.

One moonlit summer night, almost two years after they had first met, James got onto one knee and presented Rachel with a ring, which she gladly accepted. Her logical mind knew she should be afraid—hadn't she learned all too well what marriage could do to a person? But her heart told her there was no need for fear this time—James was not like Frank, would never be like Frank. And besides, Rachel realized, she was not the same girl she had been then. She had learned to stand up for herself, for what mattered to her. She knew, now, that there were more important things than living her life for others. She knew it wasn't her job to make James happy and it wasn't James' job to make her happy. And yet, knowing that he cared about her as much as she cared about him, filled her with happiness.

But if there was going to be a wedding, there were certain things that Rachel wanted to have happen. She wanted it to be the wedding that Annie and Jebediah never got to have—complete with a bustle dress for her and china plates at the reception. She made the dress, finally learning how to sew on her old treadle sewing machine. She bought many, many sets of china dishes at the second-hand store. She splurged for a pair of antique-looking lace-up boots. She found a pocket watch at an antique store for James. And James gave her a string of pearls that used to belong to his great grandmother.

They got married on the beach, in front of the cabin where it all started, surrounded by a field of daffodils. The man who performed the ceremony was a friend of James', a Native American man that had been one of the first people to greet him when he moved to the Upper Peninsula so many years ago. For Rachel, it felt as if Bill "The Bear" was in front of her again, dispersing words of wisdom from beyond time. She could almost picture Minnie standing beside him.

"Do you Rachel Annie Smith take this man, James Jebediah Jones, to be your lawfully wedded husband, for rich or poor, in sickness and health, until death do you part?"

"And then some," Rachel replied and winked at James.

"And do you, James Jebediah Jones, take this woman, Rachel Annie Smith, to be your lawfully wedded wife, for rich or poor, in sickness and health, until death do you part?"

James smiled down at Rachel. "In this lifetime, and every lifetime to come."

The end...for now.

Thank you so much for reading my book!
If you liked it, you can find my other titles
and, hopefully, leave a positive review at
www.enchantmentpress.com and/or amazon.com.
Your good words mean a lot to independent authors.

If you have any suggestions to make it better, please
send an email to enchantmentpress@gmail.com.

www.ingramcontent.com/pod-product-compliance
Lightning Source LLC
Chambersburg PA
CBHW051842170626
46807CB00003B/1301